The Executioner abandoned the trail

He tucked the carbine in close to his chest as he zigzagged down the uneven slope. The going was precarious as the ground beneath him was clotted with loose stones and small rocks. For each sure step there would be one where the ground gave way under his weight. Several times he dropped to one knee, raising welts along his thigh as he half fell, half slid his way downhill, raising a cloud of volcanic ash and dislodging the gravel around him. It was as if he'd become a one-man avalanche.

After another twenty yards, the ground abruptly fell away and he was thrown forward, off balance, into a deep recess. He struck the far edge of the gully knee-first, then with his shoulder, jarring his carbine loose. The rifle sailed past him and rolled sideways another five yards before coming to a rest. Bolan, meanwhile, slumped into the cavity, dazed. He had the presence of mind to drop as low as he could, avoiding the stream of gunfire that, moments later, skimmed past the gully's rim. As he waited for his head to clear, the Executioner reached for his web holster, unsheathing his Beretta.

He was down but not out.

MACK BOLAN ®
The Executioner

The Executioner
Don Pendleton's

LOOSE CANNON

A GOLD EAGLE BOOK FROM

W🌐RLDWIDE.

TORONTO • NEW YORK • LONDON
AMSTERDAM • PARIS • SYDNEY • HAMBURG
STOCKHOLM • ATHENS • TOKYO • MILAN
MADRID • WARSAW • BUDAPEST • AUCKLAND

Recycling programs
for this product may
not exist in your area.

First edition June 2009

ISBN-13: 978-0-373-64367-7

Special thanks and acknowledgment to
Ron Renauld for his contribution to this work.

LOOSE CANNON

The responsibility of the great states is to serve and not to dominate the world.

—Harry S. Truman,
1884–1972

When a man who holds power tries to dominate others for his own benefit, it is my responsibility to stop him.

—Mack Bolan

THE
MACK BOLAN
LEGEND

Nothing less than a war could have fashioned the destiny of the man called Mack Bolan. Bolan earned the Executioner title in the jungle hell of Vietnam.

But this soldier also wore another name—Sergeant Mercy. He was so tagged because of the compassion he showed to wounded comrades-in-arms and Vietnamese civilians.

Mack Bolan's second tour of duty ended prematurely when he was given emergency leave to return home and bury his family, victims of the Mob. Then he declared a one-man war against the Mafia.

He confronted the Families head-on from coast to coast, and soon a hope of victory began to appear. But Bolan had broken society's every rule. That same society started gunning for this elusive warrior—to no avail.

So Bolan was offered amnesty to work within the system against terrorism. This time, as an employee of Uncle Sam, Bolan became Colonel John Phoenix. With a command center at Stony Man Farm in Virginia, he and his new allies—Able Team and Phoenix Force—waged relentless war on a new adversary: the KGB.

But when his one true love, April Rose, died at the hands of the Soviet terror machine, Bolan severed all ties with Establishment authority.

Now, after a lengthy lone-wolf struggle and much soul-searching, the Executioner has agreed to enter an "arm's-length" alliance with his government once more, reserving the right to pursue personal missions in his Everlasting War.

1

Stony Man Farm, Virginia

Mack Bolan liked to start his day, whenever possible, by stretching and then going for a short jog. The routine loosened him up, eased the aches incurred from combat on a thousand battlefields and helped clear his mind so that he would feel energized and focused for whatever demands the day would bring. Of course, given the extent to which he found himself out in the field—under the gun with his life on the line—moments like this morning were more the exception than the rule. It had been weeks, in fact, since there'd been time for the Executioner to indulge in his favored regimen. So, as he loped along the inner perimeter of Stony Man Farm, breath clouding in the cool morning air, Bolan savored the moment.

He was out on the east edge of the property, where evenly spaced rows of timber trees blocked his view of the chipping mill that served as a front for the Farm's covert Annex facilities. Mottled sunlight filtered through the bird-filled poplars and a slight breeze carried with it the faint, cloying scent of fresh peaches and strawberries. Save for an occasional glimpse of the perimeter fence off to his right, Bolan had the sense of being out in the middle of nowhere, reprieved, for the moment, from his tireless commitment to stand hard and tall against those dark elements forever intent on heaving the world into a maelstrom.

As he neared the edge of the tree line, the steady, rhythmic thump of Bolan's jogging shoes on the dirt path was echoed by a similar, albeit mechanical, drone from overhead. As the sound drew closer, Bolan recognized the telltale rotor hum of the Farm's shuttle chopper. The Bell 206 was coming in from the east, a sure sign given the hour that Sensitive Operations Group Director Hal Brognola was on board, heading back from a presidential briefing in Washington. Bolan knew it was equally likely that Brognola had left the White House with news that some fresh hell had broken out at one of the world's hotspots, requiring the input of Stony Man's covert operatives to ensure that U.S. interests were not imperiled by the recent turn of events. Duty called, and with solemn intent, the Executioner cut short his morning run and changed course.

Barbara Price, Stony Man's mission controller, had emerged from the tri-level main house where she resided when not conducting business at the nearby Annex facilities. Tall, blond-haired and casually dressed in jeans and a lightweight sweater, Price had the look and bearing of a woman who knew her own mind and brooked little nonsense from anyone who might mistake her ready smile for a sign of weakness. She flashed that smile at Bolan as he approached her. He returned an equally disarming grin. The look between them spoke of shared intimacy, and though neither of them had ever so much as entertained a matrimonial notion, they acknowledged each other as soul mates, and Bolan had spent the night in Price's arms before setting out on his morning run.

Bolan gestured at the chopper, then asked Price, "Where's the fire this time?"

"LET ME RUN this back to make sure I've got it all right," Bolan said a half hour later as he sat with Brognola and Price in the Annex computer room. Brognola's face was taut with an expression of quiet intensity. Also in the room was Aaron "the Bear" Kurtzman, a burly man whose confinement to a wheelchair did little to sap a look of vitality that was only partially enhanced by his steady consumption of what others at the Farm kindly referred to as the World's Most Mediocre Coffee.

"You never get it wrong," Kurtzman told Bolan, "but this one's so convoluted a quick rehash might do us all some good."

"All right, then," Bolan said. "Two days ago in Indonesia, UNESCO found a party of seven men shot to death in a gorge in a nature preserve in Aceh Province. Less than a mile away, they came across more bodies near a Jeep that looked like it went off a mountain road after crashing into some fallen trees. They think at least a couple more men were dragged off by crocodiles."

"So far, so good," Brognola said.

"The men found in the gorge were killed by weapons found on the men who died in the Jeep crash," Bolan went on, "so the theory is the second group died while fleeing the scene of the ambush."

"And the men in the gorge were unarmed," Price added, making certain she'd pieced it all together correctly herself. "They were supposedly on a field trip trying to gauge the toll poaching had taken on the preserve's endangered species."

"Correct," Brognola said. "They were with Gerakan Aceh Merdeka."

"The Free Aceh Movement," Bolan interjected. "And the men in the Jeep were with the Ministry of the Interior. Government agents."

"The head of the ministry is running against GAM for reelection as governor of Aceh Province," Price said. She turned to Brognola. "I'm sorry, I don't remember his name."

"Noordin Zailik," Brognola said. "He's denying that the ministry agents had anything to do with ambushing the GAM people. Of course, GAM is pointing to the evidence and trying to milk the situation for all it's worth, since their guy is running neck-and-neck with Zailik in the polls."

"And their guy is Anhi Hasbrok," Bolan said. "Former head of GAM's military arm."

Kurtzman grinned at Brognola. "What'd I tell you? You run something by Striker, it's like programming it into a damn computer."

"The governor has ordered a full-scale investigation, down to going after crocodiles with tranquilizer darts on the chance they can be x-rayed for any trace of the missing G-men," the big Fed said.

"Good luck with that," Kurtzman replied.

"It's apt to be a drawn-out process," Brognola admitted. "Meanwhile, both Zailik and Hasbrok are cranking up the rhetoric to the point where Washington is worried about the area's political stability. And not just because of GAM's track record for resorting to violence."

"They're worried about JI moving in," Bolan guessed.

"Exactly," Brognola said. "Jemaah Islamiyah have been taking it on the chin lately thanks to the antiterrorist squad Densus 88, but they're not about to roll over. According to our intel, JI are replacing their cells as fast as they get knocked down, and they're hoarding whatever arms they can get off the black market. Word is they're stirring up most of the clamor in East Timor, and if they figure the time is right in Aceh, odds are they'd be quick to make a move there."

"They're backing some cleric who's running against Zailik and Hasbrok, too, right?" Kurtzman asked.

"Yes," Brognola replied, "but the guy's running a distant third. The latest polls had him at less than ten percent."

"He could wind up playing spoiler, though," Kurtzman said.

"I suppose so."

Bolan weighed the implications, then voiced his thoughts. "Any chance JI had a hand in the ambush?"

"You want to spell it out?" Brognola asked.

"It's simple," Bolan said. "If we're assuming that things

aren't the way they look, then we're saying somebody drove the ministry agents off the road, made sure they were dead, stole their weapons and used them to ambush the GAM people, then doubled back and left the weapons near the Jeep so it would look like a government hit. To pull off something like that takes a lot of precision."

"Which JI specialize at," Price added, completing the thought.

"You could have something there," Brognola conceded. "But there's another option we need to look at, too. I wanted to make sure you were clear on what went down before I brought it up, but now that you're up to speed…"

Bolan nodded. "There's always a twist."

"Unfortunately, yes." Brognola raided his attaché case for a file, which included a compact disc. "Can you cue this up for me, Bear?" he asked, handing it to Kurtzman.

Kurtzman, who oversaw the Farm's cybernetic crew, wheeled to his computer station. In seconds, he'd opened the CD's files and transferred its data onto his hard drive.

"Done," he told Brognola. "What do you want to look at first?"

"The photo file," Brognola replied.

"Coming up."

Kurtzman worked his cursor, and moments later the image of a dough-faced middle-aged man with dark hair and a well-groomed goatee filled his screen as well as one of the larger monitors imbedded on the far wall.

"Carl Ryan," Brognola said, identifying the man on the screen. "Career politico, mostly with the State Department, including a nice, long run as U.S. ambassador to Indonesia."

"Until he wound up in prison, right?" Price said. "Something to do with skimming reconstruction funds after the tsunami."

"That's right," Brognola confirmed. "He siphoned off nearly two million dollars that's been accounted for, and they think he helped himself to even more before he got caught with his hand in the cookie jar."

"I think I can see where this is headed," Bolan murmured.

"Ryan was paroled last month after serving half his sentence," Brognola explained. "He wasn't out more than a week before he disappeared."

"That would be a euphemism for 'skipped the country'," Kurtzman guessed.

"We don't have any proof yet, but that's the scenario we're working with," Brognola said. "And the thinking is that he's probably headed back to his old stomping grounds."

"To get to whatever money he managed to stash," Price said.

"Again, that's only speculation, but it would make sense," Brognola said. "And you have to consider that he's probably still connected with some key players in the islands. After all, he was ambassador for four years before the wheels came off."

"Got it," Bolan said, "but how do we figure he might be mixed up with the ambush?"

"He might not be," Brognola conceded, "but when you figure he was replaced over there by the guy who blew the whistle on him, it's fair to say he'd have an interest in seeing all hell break loose and have the new ambassador take the heat for letting things get out of hand."

"That'd be going to a lot of trouble for not much in the way of payback," Bolan said.

Brognola nodded, adding, "Or maybe the ambush is just the beginning."

2

Banda Aceh, Indonesia

"Of course we had nothing to do with it!" Noordin Zailik snapped into his speakerphone. The provincial governor, an obese man in his late fifties with dyed black hair, leaned forward in his chair and slammed his fist hard on a large oak desk where the phone rested alongside a stack of paperwork and a few objets d'art accumulated during his term in office. "The ministry agents were there because poachers had been reported in the area. For no other reason!"

"What was that noise?" a man with a calm, sonorous voice asked over the phone's speaker. Ambassador Robert Gardner was on the line from the U.S. embassy in Jakarta.

"*This* noise?" Zailik bellowed, thumping the desk a second time. "It's me cracking heads trying to find out who was behind those killings! I'm being framed and you know it!"

"I'm looking over the intel," Gardner responded, his voice taking on the tone of a school teacher whose patience was being tested by a problem student, "and I have to say, all the evidence seems to point to—"

"I don't care where the evidence points!" Zailik interrupted. "Do you really think I'd be so stupid as to place a hit on some low-level GAM lackeys? You think I don't know how something like that would backfire on me at the polls?"

The governor glared at the speakerphone, waiting for an

answer. He could imagine Gardner smirking back in his office, taking pleasure in riling him. It'd been like this from the moment Gardner had taken over as ambassador. Always so smug and condescending, just like his predecessor.

Zailik was still waiting for Gardner to respond when his personal secretary appeared in the doorway, holding a clipboard, an urgent expression on her face. The governor signaled for her to wait a moment, then leaned toward the speakerphone.

"I have an important meeting to get to," he told Gardner coldly. "Think what you want, but I'm telling you I had no hand in this and when I prove it I'll be expecting an apology!"

Zailik pressed a button on the phone's console, abruptly ending the call. He glanced back at his secretary. Ti Vohn was an attractive woman in her early thirties, conservatively dressed with her dark hair pulled back from the high cheekbones that adorned her oval face. Zailik's wife had raised a fuss when he'd hired the woman, but he'd refused to let her go. There were days, like this, when he wished his wife's jealousy had some foundation.

"What is it, Ti?" he asked, trying his best to offer the woman an inviting smile. "Good news, I hope."

"I'm sorry, sir," Vohn responded.

Zailik slumped in his chair as the woman explained that investigators combing the rain-soaked Gunung Leuser ambush sites had yet to find any evidence to refute the prevalent theory that Interior Ministry agents had carried out the GAM killings before dying when their Jeep had subsequently gone off the road as they were leaving the scene. The placement of logs across the mountain road seemed to be the work of illegal loggers who had been attempting to slide fallen trees down to the river for transport away from the park. It appeared merely coincidental that the ministry troops had crashed into the inadvertent barricade before the loggers could move the trees off the road. The investigators were still looking for the loggers but suspected they had fled the area once they realized what had happened. The rain had washed away any tracks that might have provided clues as to the direction they might have taken.

Preliminary autopsies showed that the victims had died of blunt trauma injuries likely incurred when the Jeep had plummeted into the ravine. And, as Zailik feared, little headway had been made regarding the logistical nightmare of rounding up the area's population of thousand-pound crocodiles so they could be x-rayed for any trace of those ministry agents still reported missing.

As he absorbed the news, Zailik stared dully out his window. A storm front had long passed, and morning sunlight shimmered on the black domes rising from Baiturrahman Grand Mosque, located a short walk from the governor's residence in downtown Banda Aceh. Why was Allah testing him like this? Zailik wondered fleetingly. First the tsunami, then having to deal with scandal-plagued reconstruction efforts. And now this. Whatever had happened to the dream of his governorship being a stepping stone to the presidency of all Indonesia? As it was, Zailik knew he'd be lucky to win another term as head of this godforsaken province.

Ti Vohn was eyeing Zailik expectantly when he turned back to her. He told the woman to line up a call so that he could arrange to allocate more manpower to the investigation. Somewhere out in that overgrown wilderness there had to be proof that would vindicate him, and he needed to find it as quickly as possible.

"Before I do that, there's one more thing," his secretary told him. There was a tinge of reluctance in her voice.

"More bad news, I trust," Zailik groused.

"There's a demonstration at the mosque."

Zailik shook his head miserably. "Let me guess," he ventured. "They're waving placards calling me 'GAM butcher'."

"I'm not sure of the wording, but they're holding you responsible," the secretary replied. "Word is they plan to march through town to gather more supporters, then continue the demonstration here."

"And burn me in effigy, no doubt."

Zailik eyed the clock on the wall next to him. In a couple of hours he was scheduled to fly to Takengon for a fundraising dinner. In light of events, he'd planned to cancel the appearance, but now the idea of pandering for campaign contributions seemed less burdensome than having to contend with an angry throng of GAM sympathizers.

"Round up the motorcade," he told his secretary. "I want to leave early for the airport."

"I'll make the arrangements," Vohn responded. Almost as an afterthought, she mentioned, "They're still doing repairs on the main road, so traffic might be a problem."

Without hesitation, Zailik responded, "Then we'll take the back way."

AS SHE LEFT the governor's office, Ti Vohn almost felt sorry for Zailik. The man was clearly so obsessed with proving his innocence that he wasn't thinking straight. Send more men out into the jungle? Chase after crocodiles the size of small dinosaurs hoping to find clues tucked away in their bellies? It all seemed so foolish. Why couldn't he see that his resources would be put to better use investigating likely suspects instead of going over the same ground again and again? And then there was the matter of moving up his departure time for the airport. It would be one thing if he were merely some business executive looking for his chauffeur to show up an hour earlier. But as governor there were security protocols, and given the logistics and manpower involved, to suddenly create a mad scramble to make certain the motorcade route was properly screened and readied at a moment's notice, especially under the circumstances, was foolhardy. And taking the back way was an even greater invitation to disaster. Vohn would have pointed out as much, save for the fact that she not only anticipated Zailik's desire to go to any means to avoid the demonstrators, but she had also been banking on it.

Before returning to her workstation, Vohn detoured into the ladies' room. She was the only woman working in this side of the building, but she locked the door behind her nonetheless. She retreated to one of the stalls farthest from the outer window. From her dress pocket she took a cheap prepaid cell phone and thumb-punched a memorized number. Someone answered on the seventh ring. She recognized the man's voice.

"He took the bait," she whispered. "He'll be heading for the airport within the hour."

"And you convinced him to take the back way?"

"He didn't need much convincing," Vohn said.

"Excellent," the other caller responded. "We'll be ready for him…"

Sulawesi, Indonesia

AGMED HASEM nodded approvingly as the latest group of recruits finished their training drills and fell into line before him. There were sixteen in all, ranging in age from their late teens to a couple, like Hasem, in their early thirties. They'd been worked hard and were all perspiring in the late-morning sun that beat down on the isolated camp, located five miles north of Makassar on the site of a water-treatment plant shut down years earlier when an upgraded facility had been completed closer to the city.

"Well done, praise Allah," he told them. "Jemaah Islamiyah is blessed to have men of such caliber ready to devote themselves to our noble cause."

In truth, Hasem was somewhat disappointed in the effort he'd seen. Most of the recruits were clumsy and far more winded from their exertions than he would have liked. But he'd found over the years that it was better to stroke the egos of those looking to join his fold than to play drill sergeant. Fill them with pride, food and constant indoctrination about the glory of martyrdom and there was a better chance they would be ready to lay down their lives on the suicide missions that were Hasem's preferred modus operandi.

And, too, there was the matter of replenishing the ranks following a month when JI had seen more than a dozen men killed or imprisoned in raids on camps across the Java Sea in Larantuka and Maumere. The raids, carried out by Densus 88 antiterror squads, had, like countless other sweeps over the past five years, been widely publicized in the media, giving the impression that Jemaah Islamiyah was on the ropes and facing eradication. Hasem took issue with the assessment but there was no denying that bad press had taken its toll on recruitment. Gone were the days when JI routinely turned away fringe candidates for the organization. Now, Hasem and other field commanders had been forced to become more solicitous and less discriminating.

Things would change soon, though, Hasem reasoned. Even as he was exhorting the recruits, the charismatic leader knew that JI teams in Banda Aceh were preparing to launch what would be the first in a series of counterstrikes against Densus 88. If all went well, when the dust settled, JI's reputation would be such that once again they would be able to pick and choose from the swelling ranks of those eager to join the cause. For now, however, Hasem would make do with what he had.

Hasem lectured his minions a few minutes longer, giving the men a well-practiced spiel heavy on references to Allah and laden with vitriol demonizing the United States as the Great Satan. Much was made, too, of the threat posed by secular leaders throughout the islands—men like Governor Zailik of Aceh Province—who took a hardline stance against Islamic fundamentalists. Those local politicians, to Hasem's way of thinking, were every bit a hindrance to what JI stood for as the Americans and their European counterparts. Indonesia, after all, contained the highest Muslim concentration in the world. What better place for Islam to flourish and lay the groundwork for a long-overdue return to global prominence?

A breeze rustled through the camp, and as the recruits detected the smell of fried rice and roast goat coming from the kitchens set up inside the former treatment plant, Hasem could see the men's attention beginning to waver. He quickly wrapped up his remarks, then sent the men to eat.

A truck had pulled up to the site, parking near Hasem's quarters, a rusting Quonset hut set back at the edge of the clearing. Hasem went to check on things, catching up with the driver as he was circling around the truck.

"Did you get it?" he asked.

"See for yourself," the driver told him. He opened the rear doors of the truck, revealing an oblong wooden crate the size of a small coffin. The lid was unfastened, and when Hasem raised it, he smiled. Laid out in neat rows within the crate where thin slabs of Semtec. Once placed in the lining of snug vests worn beneath loose clothing, the plastic explosives would be difficult to detect to the visible eye. As such, they would be a far better choice for suicide missions than dynamite sticks or the other, bulkier explosive materials JI had been forced to rely on, thanks to Densus 88's clampdown on the black market.

"Excellent," Hasem said, placing the lid back on the crate. He told the driver to wait while he went for his payment, then headed toward the nearby hut. He was met in the doorway by one of his lieutenants, Guikin Daeng, a sallow, sneering man in his late twenties.

"I was just coming to track you down," Daeng told Hasem. "We just received word from our team in Banda Aceh. Governor Zailik is setting out early for the airport, just as we hoped."

"Our little demonstration scared him out of his cozy little nest?" Hasem asked.

Daeng nodded, then squawked like a chicken and laughed.

"Out of the frying pan," Hasem intoned. "Into the fire…"

Nearly twenty-one hours after its departure from a private airfield in Washington D.C., the Cessna Citation X jet carrying Mack Bolan dropped through the cloud cover veiling the Strait of Malacca, giving the Executioner a glimpse of Banda Aceh. He was seated in the lavishly appointed eight-seat passenger cabin, his view out the right window only partially obstructed by the jet's sub-mounted wing. The jet was RICCO booty recently claimed by the government after the arrest and conviction of a high-rolling Chicago drug dealer.

The Executioner wasn't the only passenger aboard the jet.

"Y'know, I could get used to this," John "Cowboy" Kissinger drawled from the seat next to Bolan. Legs stretched out, the Stony Man weaponsmith had his feet propped on a foldout table that also held the remains of a gourmet breakfast he'd put together in the jet's galley after sleeping most of the trip with his leather-and-suede chair fully reclined. "Only thing missing was some foxy stewardess ready to initiate me into the Mile-High Club."

"Maybe next time," Bolan deadpanned.

Some years back, Kissinger had left his career as a DEA field agent to join the covert ops team at Stony Man Farm. The original plan had been for him to stay on-site and oversee the acquisition and maintenance of the vast arsenal stockpiled in an outbuilding near the main quarters, and he'd excelled at both functions while finding time to tinker with new prototypes and modify existing weapons to improve performance and reliability in the battlefield. In time, though, he'd come to miss taking on the enemy firsthand, and whenever Hal Brognola or Barbara Price found themselves shorthanded when doling out assignments, Kissinger was usually the first to volunteer. Conversely, whenever Bolan felt the need for backup going into a mission, he invariably turned to Cowboy, as well as the pilot currently minding the Citation's controls.

"Okay, boys and girls," Jack Grimaldi called out over the intercom as the jet continued its descent toward the airport located six miles inland from Banda Aceh. "You know the drill. Seats up, belts on, and stash away anything you don't want pinballing around the compartment should I suddenly forget what the hell I'm doing and wind up dribbling this sucker across the landing strip."

Kissinger got up long enough to take his and Bolan's breakfast trays back to the galley, then strapped himself in for landing. He saw the Executioner still staring out the portal beside him.

"Already looking for that needle in the haystack, eh?"

"Something like that," Bolan replied.

In truth, though, the Executioner's attention was focused on a flurry of activity around one of the far hangars, where a handful of armed men in combat fatigues were crossing the tarmac toward where crews were hastily fuelling what looked to be a vintage Vietnam-era Huey. A pair of military Jeeps had pulled up alongside the combat chopper as well, ready to take on a few more passengers. Kissinger finally glanced out the window and caught a glimpse of the pandemonium.

"That's our hangar, isn't it?" he asked Bolan.

Bolan nodded as he continued to monitor the activity. "I have a feeling they're up to something besides rolling out the red carpet...."

"NICE TIMING, MATE," Shelby Ferstera told Bolan ten minutes later as the Executioner deplaned. "You want to hit the ground running, you've come to the right place."

Ferstera was a tall, broad-shouldered Australian in his early forties. A former member of that country's elite Special Forces, Ferstera now served as field commander for Densus 88, eighty-eight being the number of Australians killed during the deadly 2002 bombings in downtown Bali. Ferstera had lost a sister in that bloodbath, so he'd been among the first to volunteer for the counterterrorist unit, joining forces with several U.S. Delta Force veterans and a handful of CIA operatives, who, with the help of well-trained Indonesian nationals, had been instrumental in thwarting Jemaah Islamiyah's efforts to surpass the carnage wreaked in the Balinese incident. Their tactics over the years had been as effective as they had been controversial, resulting in the arrest of several thousand JI conspirators and the deaths of several hundred others.

Still, Ferstera knew the enemy was far from defeated, and he was not the sort of man to let pride get in the way of welcoming another ally in the fight. He'd been given the standard cover story that Bolan, under the alias of Matt Cooper, and his crew were special agents for the Justice Department, but the Aussie knew better. When told by his CIA colleagues not to pry into Cooper's background, Ferstera felt certain that by sending these men to help with the situation in the islands, the U.S. had decided to play an ace stashed up its sleeve.

For his part, Bolan at first misinterpreted the commando's greeting.

"You found Ryan?" the Executioner asked as he shook the Australian's hand.

"We'll give you a hand with that in good time," Ferstera assured Bolan. "Meantime, how about a little warm-up exercise?"

Bolan stared past Ferstera at the Huey and the waiting

Jeeps. If Ryan had not yet shown up on their radar, he knew enough about Densus 88 to know who they were preparing to go after. "JI?"

Ferstera nodded. "We've got an informant who says they staged a rally in town so they could flush the governor from his quarters. He's on his way here, and he left without a full security clearance. Worse yet, he's taking the back way to avoid traffic. My money says he's heading for trouble."

The situation seemed far afield from Bolan's intended mission, but he wasn't about to back away from Ferstera's request. Once Grimaldi and Kissinger caught up with him, he quickly relayed the news, then turned back to Ferstera and asked, "Where do you want us?"

DUE TO THE LAST-MINUTE change in the governor's itinerary, only two of the intended six motorcycle patrol officers were available to escort Noordin Zailik when he prepared to leave his government quarters in a chauffeured Lincoln Town Car. The police helicopter scheduled to provide aerial support at the original departure time was en route from an assignment in nearby Lheue. It was expected to catch up with the governor by the time he reached the back country road serving as his alternate route to the airport. In the meantime, the down-sized motorcade took a circuitous route through the city, taking care to avoid Baiturrahman Grand Mosque as well as main thoroughfares or any other area where protestors were likely to be gathered.

Zailik was too preoccupied with other matters to give much thought to his compromised security. He'd been on the phone since the moment he'd sat down in the car, and now, miles later, as he closed his cell phone after speaking with Provincial Intelligence Director Sinso Dujara, Zailik frowned to himself. Something about Dujara's demeanor during the call had seemed off. Dujara was, by nature, both contentious and territorial, and Zailik had expected the man to bristle at the suggestion that not enough was being done to ferret out clues regarding the deadly incidents in Gunung Leuser. Instead of being defensive, however, Dujara had gone so far as to apologize for the lack of progress in the investigation and welcomed Zailik's suggestion to allot more manpower to the task. An apology? A gesture of humility from the most arrogant man in his makeshift cabinet? It just wasn't like Dujara. Something wasn't right.

Or maybe I'm just being paranoid, Zailik thought.

He tried to put the matter out of his mind as he fished through his coat pocket, taking out the notes he'd been working on for his upcoming fund-raiser speech in Takengon. He was glad that he'd decided not to cancel the appearance, which he knew could have a strong bearing on the final stretch of the governor's race.

Takengon, located in the center of the province on the shores of Laut Tawar Lake, had long had aspirations of becoming a tourist mecca, but most travel guides still balked at recommending the area based on years of bloody skirmishes in the vicinity, most of them involving GAM separatists. In truth, there had been no political violence in the area since the tsunami. But the stigma remained, and as such Takengon's movers and shakers were adamantly opposed to the gubernatorial candidacy of Anhi Hasbrok, who'd commandeered GAM forces in most of the battles waged near the aspiring resort. And since third-party candidate Islamic cleric Nyak Lamm had denounced leisure pursuits such as water-skiing and sunbathing as degenerate Western vices, Zailik was certain he'd be able to replenish his campaign coffers by assuring the locals that he remained a steadfast champion of tourism as well as a foe of clerical involvement in regional politics.

The governor quickly lost himself in his speechwriting, and it wasn't until his chauffeur cursed under his breath that Zailik took his mind off the task long enough to glimpse out the window. In an instant, he realized it may have been a mistake to take the back way to the airport.

The motorcade was passing along a remote, two-lane stretch of roadway that separated a partially completed low-income housing development from a rolling meadow overrun by tents and clapboard shanties where thousands of displaced residents of Banda Aceh had been living in squalor and discontent as they waited for construction on the new homes to be completed. The development was two years behind schedule, thanks largely to the former U.S. ambassador's pilfering of tsunami relief funds. However, many of the indigents held Zailik responsible for their dire straits, and it seemed someone had leaked word that he would be passing through the area. Several dozen people had wandered out from the tenement and taken up positions along the road, where they jeered and waved their arms angrily at the approaching motorcade. The crowd was made up primarily of men, though there were a handful of women and several boys in their early teens. As the car drew closer, they collectively drifted out onto the road, forming a human barricade.

"So much for avoiding demonstrators," Zailik mused as he eyed the throng. The chauffeur slowed the car and the patrolman who'd been riding behind them pulled around to the front, joining his counterpart. They stopped their motorcycles at an angle, forming a protective V behind which the governor's car eased to a halt twenty yards shy of the protestors. Beyond the demonstrators, Zailik saw two cars approaching from the direction of the airport. Apparently dissuaded by the commotion, both drivers slowed and made quick U-turns, leaving the confrontation behind.

Zailik fumed. He wanted to get out and confront his detractors. What business did they have making him a scapegoat for their miseries? The tsunami hadn't been his fault, and when Ambassador Ryan's wholesale embezzlement had come to light, it had been Zailik who'd spearheaded efforts to secure relief funding elsewhere. If not for him, the lot across the road would still be nothing more than a pad of dirt instead of a development where there were at least signs of forward progress.

The governor's indignation was quickly tempered when a piece of rotten fruit splattered against the tinted windshield he was looking through. Zailik instinctively recoiled, then let out a gasp when the next projectile—a rock the size of a baseball—struck the window. The glass was bulletproof and the rock left only small, weblike cracks, but Zailik suddenly realized he was facing more than a mere inconvenience. Casting aside his speech notes, the governor quickly grabbed his cell phone. Too flustered to dial a number, he instead pressed Redial, putting a call through to Intelligence Director Dujara. The official had little to do with the governor's security arrangements, but Zailik was desperate.

"There's a mob on the road to the airport!" he bellowed once Dujara picked up. "They're after me...!"

4

The two motorcycle officers were brothers. Muhtar Yeilam, the oldest by three years, had joined the Banda Aceh police force straight out of college and distinguished himself as a patrol officer during the tsunami, saving a handful of lives and helping to maintain order in the storm's traumatic aftermath. Muhtar's example—along with the ceremony where he'd been decorated for heroism—had inspired his younger brother to follow in his footsteps. In three months Ashar would have his first year under his belt.

Muhtar had pulled strings to get his brother assigned to the governor's detail, and this was the first time they'd worked together. Escorting Governor Zailik to the airport was a routine, inconsequential assignment. While waiting for the motorcade to get underway less than an hour earlier, the brothers had been joking with one another, enjoying their sibling camaraderie as they argued over who would be the first to get laid after they hit the discos later that night.

Suddenly, everything had changed.

"I thought this was supposed to be a walk in the park," Ashar said. It was meant to be a wisecrack, but there was an edge in his voice. He idled his motorcycle and planted his boots on the road as he grabbed for the police-issue 9 mm automatic pistol nestled in its holster.

Muhtar had his gun out and was pointing it at the mob. Like Ashar, he remained on his bike, left hand lightly on the clutch, ready to get back in gear at a moment's notice. He glanced quickly over at his brother. Save for a couple of high-speed chases, this was Ashar's first true taste of danger since he'd received his badge. Muhtar could sense a glimmer of fear in his brother's demeanor.

"I guess some parks aren't as safe as others," Muhtar quipped, trying to sound nonchalant and put his brother at ease.

The mob before them slowly began to fan out. Most of the protestors had already been unnerved by the sight of the armed policemen. They receded en masse to the shoulder. However, several men and one young boy split off from the group and began to circle around the governor's car as if hoping to reach the vehicle from behind. Meanwhile, nearly a dozen protestors—many of them women and young boys—held their ground in front of the motorcade, linking arms to form a human chain that stretched across the entire width of the road and out onto the shoulder. Those at the end of the line clutched rocks slightly larger than the one that had already been thrown.

"We want the governor!" one of the women shouted at the two officers.

"Tell him to show his face!" another cried out.

Muhtar lowered his gun slightly and forced himself to remain calm. He ignored their demands but tried to reason with them.

"Please," he said, trying to make eye contact with as many of the demonstrators as he could, "there's no sense letting this get out of hand. Just drop the rocks and move away from the road."

The plea fell on deaf ears. Those blocking the road stayed where they were, arms entwined, and continued to demand an audience with Zailik.

Ashar was less tactful than his brother when he swiveled astride his bike to contend with those making a move toward the car's unprotected rear flank.

"Don't even think about it!" he shouted.

When the stray demonstrators ignored him and continued

toward the car, Ashar fired a warning shot over their heads. Startled, the group scrambled back. One man stumbled into another, knocking loose a rock the second man had been preparing to throw. Together, they retreated to the shoulder and rejoined the others, content, for the moment at least, to merely hurl insults at the man inside the car.

"The governor drives in a fancy limousine while we have no running water!" one taunted. "When will we have new homes instead of having to live out of tents and boxes?"

Another bellowed, "And what about those GAM workers he had executed the other night? Explain that, Governor!"

"If you have a problem with the governor, take it up at the ballot box!" Ashar snapped. "Not here!"

Muhtar whirled on his bike and shouted at his brother, "Don't antagonize them! Just do your job!"

Ashar nodded and fell silent. Muhtar could see that his brother's gun hand was trembling slightly, as were his knees, which were pressed close to the sides of his idling motorcycle. Muhtar knew that Ashar had gone through crowd-control drills during his training at the police academy, but in the heat of the moment his brother had clearly reverted to his hothead instincts.

"Just relax, Ashie," Muhtar called out. "Don't rile them up and we'll get through this."

Ashar continued to nod, but Muhtar was concerned. If his brother's uneasiness was as obvious to the mob as it was to him, things could easily go from bad to worse in an instant.

By now a small delivery truck and a minivan were coming up behind the governor's car. Both vehicles slowed to a stop. The minivan's driver, like those in the cars that moments ago had been coming from the other direction, quickly assessed the situation and thought better of trying to move past the confrontation. Veering off the road for a moment, the van turned around and doubled back toward Banda Aceh. The driver of the truck was apparently not about to let matters throw him off schedule. After the van had passed him, he drove forward, picking up speed as he moved into the oncoming lane as if intent on passing the governor's car. However, when a hurled rock smashed through the passenger side of the front windshield, just missing him, the man had second thoughts. He slammed on his brakes, then jammed the truck into Reverse and backed down the road a good thirty yards before making a quick three-point turn. Like the driver of the minivan before him, he retraced his route back to the city.

The motorcycle officers, meanwhile, remained on their bikes and kept a wary vigil over the protestors. Pistols outstretched before them, they fanned the weapons steadily from side to side in an effort to keep the mob at bay. It looked to Muhtar as if he'd gotten through to his brother. Ashar's visible fidgeting had stopped and he seemed locked in to his police mentality, forearms rigid as he continued to keep his gun trained on the demonstrators. Muhtar was relieved. Though they were clearly outnumbered, he felt certain they would keep the upper hand so long as they gave the sense of being in control.

There was, however, the matter of the human chain that continued to block their way to the airport. No one had moved, and the man on the right end of the chain was still holding the rock Muhtar had told him to drop. The man at the other end of the line had only partially complied with the order; his rock had gone through the windshield of the now-retreating delivery truck.

"Put the rock down and everyone move off the road!" Muhtar told the group again, this time with more authority.

The demonstrators held their ground.

"We want answers!" one of the women shouted, raising her shrill voice to make certain the mob could hear it over the drone of the motorcycles. She pointed past the officers at the car, adding, "Tell that coward to show his face and give him to us!"

As she'd hoped, the woman's harangue rallied the mob. Once again they began to chant and jeer. Another rock and several ears of corn bounded off the car, and Muhtar grimaced when a small, flat stone struck him squarely on the shoulder.

"Zailik's a coward!" someone in the crowd howled. Some began to clap their hands in rhythm, as if at a sporting event. "Zailik's a coward! Zailik's a coward!"

Drawn by the commotion, more residents of the tent city began to emerge from their dingy quarters and head toward the road. Some had already grabbed tools and makeshift clubs, and several others paused along the way to pick up more rocks.

"Not good," Muhtar murmured under his breath, refusing to visibly acknowledge the stinging welt on his shoulder.

Concerned the balance would soon shift out of their favor, the two brothers, without taking their eyes off the growing mob, spoke hurriedly to one another, trying to determine the best course of action. There was no way they were going to let Zailik out of the car—it was too dangerous and both brothers doubted there would be anything the governor could say to diffuse the situation. Ashar thought their best chance was to proceed with the motorcade in hopes the demonstrators would scramble out of the way once they realized their bluff was being called. Muhtar, however, was concerned about the possible ramifications if the crowd failed to move and some of them wound up being struck by their motorcycles.

"They put women and children out there for a reason," Muhtar explained. "We run in to any of them and we'll have a riot on our hands."

"If we wait around for this mob to get any larger, all hell is going to break loose anyway," Ashar countered, allowing his anger and frustration to override his earlier fears. "I say we head out and pick up speed as fast as we can, and whatever happens—"

"Wait!" Muhtar held a hand up to silence his brother. He stole a glance over his shoulder and peered back over the roof of the car. Ashar did the same.

"Finally!" the younger brother called out.

The crowd's attention had been diverted as well, and the chanting quickly tapered off as they stared down the road. Heading toward them, swooping low as it approached from the city, was the overdue police helicopter.

"Not a moment too soon," Muhtar intoned.

The sense of an impending riot abated as the chopper drew nearer. Moments later, there were worried murmurs among those in the crowd when they spotted a second, larger helicopter heading toward them from the direction of the airport. Beneath the massive Huey, a pair of Jeeps could also be seen racing along the road, filled with armed commandos. As if to make certain their approach had not gone unnoticed, several men in the lead Jeep fired warning shots with their assault rifles, gouging divots from the road's shoulder just shy of where the protestors were gathered. The crowd took notice and quickly fell back on itself. Some of the latecomers turned heel and fled back toward the tent city. Even those still out on the roadway were given pause; the chain was broken as they turned to face the armed force that had just sucked the life from their demonstration.

"Densus 88," Ashar Yeilam exclaimed with an almost reverential sense of wonder. He eyed Shelby Ferstera's hallowed contingent as if he were some refugee from a comic book greeting the unexpected arrival of superheroes as a sure sign that soon all would be right with the world.

Though to a lesser degree, Muhtar shared his brother's sentiment. He could barely keep himself from smiling as he kept his gun trained on the now-subdued mob. That was too close, he thought to himself.

SHORTLY AFTER THE FIRST ROCK had struck the windshield, Noordin Zailik's chauffeur had advised him to lie low in the backseat. The governor had been quick to oblige, to an extent. Zailik had felt that lying across the seat would have only made him feel more helpless and vulnerable, so he'd compromised by half-crouching, half-kneeling between the seats, his attention divided between watching the drama unfold outside and draining his cell phone in an effort to get someone—anyone—to come to his rescue before the situation on the blocked roadway got further out of hand. Intelligence Director Dujara had transferred his initial call to Banda Aceh's police chief, Irwandi Alkihn, who'd assured Zailik the helicopter assigned to him was on the way and that, furthermore, a Densus 88 unit stationed at the airport was taking action to fill the breach Zailik himself had created by leaving for the airport ahead of schedule.

As the governor had waited for the reinforcements, his anxiety increased with every passing second. After the second barrage of debris struck the car, Zailik had sunk lower between the seats until he was no longer able to peer out the windows. The chauffeur had tried to keep him apprised of what was happening outside the vehicle, but as he listened to the almost surreal play-by-play, Zailik found himself distracted. Over and over, his mind kept playing back the chain of events that had led to his predicament. He'd already come to realize that much of it was his own doing, but he was equally certain there was blame to be laid elsewhere, and as he thought back, he made a mental note of everyone who'd been privy to the alterations in his itinerary. Only a handful of people had known of the route change in time to have been able to forewarn the tent dwellers that he was headed their way. He'd just spoken with two of them, Dujara and Alkihn, but however much he personally disliked both men, Zailik had known them both for years and felt their loyalty was beyond reproach. His suspicions led him elsewhere; to the person who'd prompted his decision to take the back way in the first place.

Zailik wanted to believe there was no way Ti Vohn could have duped him into harm's way—or that he could have allowed himself to be so easily led, for that matter—but the more he'd thought about it, the more convinced he'd become that his personal secretary, whom he'd known for all of eight months, was indeed the culprit.

The realization struck a strange chord inside the governor. Rather than viewing Ti Vohn's betrayal in terms of the crisis it had gotten him into, Zailik instead found himself fixating on what a field day his wife would have when she learned the news. She'd warned him about the woman, after all, and though it had been for the wrong reasons, Zailik knew she would never let him live this down.

Driven by his wounded pride and ignoring the fact that he might not live long enough to incur his wife's scorn, Zailik had become obsessed with trying to reach Ti Vohn on his cell phone. He was convinced that once she heard his voice, her startled response would betray her, just as she'd betrayed him. At that moment nothing seemed more important to him than verifying his suspicions.

Zailik had become oblivious to the ebb and flow of the confrontation taking place outside the car. Balled up behind the driver's seat, all he could hear was the mad pulsing of blood rushing through his temples and the frantic stabbing of his thumb against the cell-phone keypad, followed time and again by a recorded message where his secretary explained that she was unable to answer the phone.

"Pick up, damn you!" Zailik seethed after the fifth time he'd dialed both her work and personal numbers.

He was about to dial yet again when the entire car began to shake and wobble. Zailik could hear a loud thundering outside the vehicle. Forced back to reality, Zailik's first thought was that the demonstrators had stormed the car and were attempting to overturn it. But as he was unfolding himself from his crouch, he detected motion through the sunroof overhead and glanced up. It was then he realized the police helicopter had arrived and was hovering directly above him, using its intense rotor wash to drive back the demonstrators who'd yet to stray from the road.

Looking out the front windshield, Zailik could see the motorcycle officers hunched low over their bikes, uniforms snapping in the fierce downdraft as the chopper eased past them, then tilted slightly so that the demonstrators caught the full brunt of the whirlwind. Many of the tent dwellers lost their footing and tumbled backward, then found themselves rolling across the tarmac toward the shoulder of the road.

"I think you just lost a few votes," the chauffeur called out as he prepared to shift the car back into gear. "But at least now we'll be able to get you to the airport...."

MACK BOLAN WAS RIDING shotgun in the second of the two Jeeps racing down the road from the airport. Jack Grimaldi was behind the wheel and John Kissinger was in the back along with one of the Densus 88 commandos, Daud Umar, a 37-year-old native of Banda Aceh.

"So far, so good," Grimaldi said as he watched the Huey bank toward the mob. Like the police chopper, the larger aircraft was using its rotor wash to keep the protestors off the road. Clouds of dust rose into the air, providing a protective screen as the motorcade began to inch forward. The lead Jeep had stopped thirty yards ahead of the motorcycle officers. Shelby Ferstera stood in the front seat, gesturing to the motorcycle cops that the Jeep would turn around once the motorcade had passed and would follow as they proceeded to the airport.

Watching things play out, Bolan had a sense that something was wrong. It was all going far too smoothly. Ferstera's informant, after all, had said that Jemaah Islamiyah had planned to go after the governor, and from what he knew of the terrorist sect, he thought their game plan would have consisted of more than setting loose a rock-throwing mob.

"Keep an eye on the crowd," he called out over his shoulder.

"On it," Kissinger replied. He was already putting to use a pair of high-powered binoculars. "It's a little hard, though, with all that dust."

Bolan turned his attention to the other side of the road, where the skeletal wooden frames of several hundred homes spread out across a series of unpaved streets. A few of the structures closest to the road were nearer to completion than the others, their inner walls hammered into place with foil-backed insulation strips secured between the studs. A handful of construction vehicles was parked nearby, but there was no sign of activity. Bolan had binoculars, too, and he used them to take a closer look at one of the bulldozers situated between a Dumpster and a large stack of lumber. Half-hidden behind the earthmover's large front scoop, the Executioner spotted a body sprawled across the dirt.

He was about to pass along his findings when, out of the corner of his eye, he saw a thin ribbon of smoke trail out from a second-story window of one of the homes near the road. A split second later, the police helicopter disintegrated in a fireball, showering the road with debris.

"A trap," Bolan shouted, even as a second missile streaked through the air, broadsiding the Huey. In an instant, Governor Zailik lost his aerial support, and the Executioner knew his instincts had been correct.

5

Once the last fiery remains of the two downed helicopters had crashed onto the roadway between his Jeep and the governor's motorcade, Shelby Ferstera fought off his shock and cursed. Jemaah Islamiyah had lured him into an ambush and now, in the blink of an eye, more than a dozen of his best men were gone. He could see a few of them scattered amid the flaming shrapnel, lifeless bodies rent and torn by the force of the explosion. Some were engulfed in flames, others spattered with blood, all of them missing limbs so that they looked like the remains of storefront mannequins that had been run through a threshing machine. There was nothing to be done for them other than to see to it that they had not died in vain. And despite the devastating blow to his ranks, Ferstera was determined to carry out Densus 88's mission and ensure the governor's safety. To do that, however, he had to make certain the rest of his men were not slaughtered by the enemy.

"Out of the Jeep and take cover!" he commanded, bolting from the vehicle. The surviving commandos followed suit, and not a moment too soon. Even as they were flattening themselves against the roadway, a stream of gunfire strafed over their heads and pelted the Jeep. The shots were coming from the direction of the tent city, so Ferstera crawled around to the far side of the vehicle. His men were right behind him. Three of them made it. A fourth caught a hail of bullets and slumped to the roadway, dead by the time his face struck the asphalt.

"Jackals!" Ferstera shouted.

He glanced quickly behind him. The Americans in the other Jeep had detoured from the road and were headed toward the housing development. They were veering to and fro to make themselves less of a target for the JI snipers firing from the upper floor of one of the uncompleted homes. Smoke and flames from the downed Huey's charred fuselage blocked Ferstera's view of those snipers, but he trusted that meant the enemy was similarly unable to take aim his way, allowing his men to focus on the gunners across the road.

Readying his M-16, Ferstera rose to one knee and peered over the Jeep's hood. Through the rifle's scope he was able to pinpoint a sniper positioned behind a large boulder on a raised knoll just beyond the tent city. The gunman had spent his ammo and was slamming a fresh cartridge into his rifle. He was a long way off, barely within range of Ferstera's M-16, but the Aussie was an expert marksman and proved it as he cut loose with a burst that streaked above the rocks and found home in the enemy's chest, taking the sniper down.

Wasting no time on self-congratulation, Ferstera scanned the knoll for more targets. He knew the playing field was a long way from being leveled....

MUHTAR YEILAM was knocked unconscious when a chunk of the obliterated police chopper crashed down on him. When he came to moments later, he was lying on the road next to his toppled motorcycle, fighting off a wave of nausea brought on by the stench of raw fuel and charred flesh. A searing, knife-like pain gnawed at his skull. Reflexively, he grabbed at his helmet and pried it off his head. The pain abated quickly as he noticed that the helmet had cracked almost in two while absorbing the impact of the fallen debris, which lay a few feet away, smoldering next to a severed arm. Staring past the grisly sight, Muhtar saw that the road was strewn with carnage.

Beyond his field of vision, he could hear screams and gunfire and the flap of loose clothing as people fled in all directions, trying to take themselves out of the line of fire.

When he tried to rise, Muhtar became aware of a tingling numbness in his legs. Glancing down, he saw blood seeping through his right pantleg up high near his hip. He wasn't sure what had caused the wound, but he knew he had to stop the bleeding. As he reached down, a sudden, aching weariness washed over him him, and he could feel himself on the verge of passing out again.

"No!" he gasped, shaking his head, fighting to remain conscious.

Then he thought of his brother.

"Ashar," he murmured, groaning at the monumental effort it took as he rolled over and tried to get up. He collapsed back onto the roadway. He'd moved enough that he could see Ashar, however. His younger brother had been knocked off his motorcycle as well, but the blow had been less severe, as Ashar was on his feet, crouched near the front grille of the governor's car, trading shots with an assailant firing down at him from one of the half-built homes off to his right. A group of commandos had entered the housing project and were heading toward the house where the shots originated.

"Need to help," Muhtar moaned to himself.

He ignored the bleeding in his leg and looked around him. His service pistol lay a few feet away on the road next to his toppled bike. Drawing in a deep breath, he rallied his strength and willed himself to roll toward the gun, then reached out and slowly closed his fingers around it.

Straining, Muhtar turned onto his other side and propped himself up slightly with his free arm. He looked back down at his legs; they were still numb and the bloodstain on his hip was spreading. He took solace, though, when he realized he could wriggle both his feet. *Not paralyzed*, he thought. He knew he was probably in shock and convinced himself that the numbness would soon go. He would tend to the bleeding later, but for now he wanted to do what he could to help his brother protect the governor, who, Muhtar assumed, was still alive inside the car.

From his new position, Muhtar could see across the road, where there was a flurry of commotion. Most of the demonstrators had retreated back toward the tent city, but a handful of men stood just off the shoulder, hunched in a tight circle like football players huddling to discuss their next play. Something about their demeanor—they way they'd turned their backs on the pandemonium around them—put Muhtar on alert.

His suspicions were borne out when, a few seconds later, the men suddenly turned away from each other, eyes on the governor's car. Remaining in a tight formation, they strode purposefully out onto the road, heading toward the vehicle. Muhtar could see that they were making an effort to shield one man in particular. When he saw the man reaching under the folds of his loose shirt, adrenaline spiked through his veins, giving him the strength to let out a plaintive cry.

"Ashar!" Muhtar shouted to his brother. "Behind you! They have a bomb!"

ASHAR YEILAM WHIRLED at the sound of his brother's voice. Muhtar had managed to get a shot off before blacking out, and one of the men approaching the governor's car dropped to the road. The others continued forward, closing ranks to protect the man in the middle of the formation. Shelby Ferstera had also been alerted by Muhtar's cry and two more men went down when the Aussie cut loose with his M-16. Ashar took out a fourth with the last round in his weapon. That left three men, however, including the one fumbling with the bomb concealed beneath his loose shirt. They reached the car and pressed themselves against the passenger side of the vehicle.

There was no time for Ashar to reload. Casting the gun aside, he raised one foot onto the front bumper of the car, then pushed off with the other and leapt up onto the hood. As his forward momentum carried him toward the three demonstrators, Ashar extended his arms. The other men were crowded together enough that he was able to collide with all three of them, knocking them away from the car. As he fell to road, the young police officer managed to drag down two of the men, including the bomber.

But it wasn't enough.

Though shaken and lying on his back, the bomber quickly regained his wits and grabbed at the detonator wired to the sticks of dynamite strapped to his chest. With a malignant grin, he eyed Ashar, who was an arm's length away, preparing to lunge..

"Praise Allah!" the bomber cried out, triggering the detonator.

THE EXECUTIONER and his colleagues were thirty yards from the partially built home the JI snipers were firing from. "Try to hotwire the bulldozer and put it to use!" Bolan shouted to Grimaldi.

The pilot nodded and was headed toward the earthmover when a violent explosion shook the ground under his feet, throwing him off balance. Bolan felt it, too. He crouched behind a Jeep, M-16 at the ready, and glanced over his shoulder, just in time to see the governor's car fly into the air and slam back onto the road, landing on its roof.. There was a small crater in the road where the bomb had gone off. Nearby, a fresh heap of corpses lay in mangled ruin.

"Suicide bomber," John Kissinger murmured, hunched next to Bolan behind the Jeep.

Bolan nodded gravely, ears ringing from the explosion. One side of the governor's car had been caved in by the bomb's force, but he thought there was a chance the governor might have survived the blast. If so, Zailik would have to wait to be rescued. Shelby Ferstera's surviving commandos had their hands full contending with snipers on the hill behind the tent city, and when gunfire coming from a second house peppered his Jeep, Bolan knew that he was locked into his own battlefield.

Daud Umar, the Densus 88 member rounding out Bolan's crew, had taken cover behind a stack of lumber just to the right of the Jeep. He fired at the enemy gunners in the second house, then pulled back when a return volley splintered the two-by-fours.

"Give 'em a grenade!" Bolan shouted.

Umar nodded, grabbing for an M6 clipped to his ammo belt. He waited out another round from the JI gunners, then thumbed the pin free and twisted his body, heaving the grenade. His aim was off, but not by much. The grenade exploded as it struck the loose dirt just in front of the house where the sniper was embedded.

The front door flew off its hinges and a dust cloud bloomed into the air, mixing with smoke given off by the blast. Bolan doubted the enemy inside the house had been taken out, but he figured they'd at least been distracted.

"Now!" he called out, breaking clear of the Jeep.

Together, Bolan and Kissinger rushed the house, using the dust cloud to mask their approach. Kissinger, like Bolan, had been issued an M-16, but his assault rifle came equipped with an under-barrel M-203 grenade launcher. As the dust began to settle, he stopped and planted himself behind a bulky, two-wheeled rototiller, shifting his trigger finger from the carbine to the launcher.

"Go wide!" he shouted to Bolan, waving to his left.

The Executioner veered away from Kissinger, following the dust cloud as it began to drift. Kissinger took aim at the house, peering through the haze. Once he could make out the framework of the ground-floor window, he fired. A 40 mm grenade *whooshed* from the launcher and finished off the job Daud Umar had started, penetrating the house before it detonated.

Bolan didn't wait to see if the blast had neutralized the enemy. Cutting toward the house, he set his sights on the front door, ready to finish the job.

FIFTY YARDS AWAY, Grimaldi had already scrambled past the dead man next to the bulldozer and climbed up to the driver's compartment. There was blood on the seat and when Grimaldi glanced down to his right, he spotted another slain worker sprawled on the ground near the treads. The man had apparently been gunned down while at the controls, because there were keys in the ignition, saving Grimaldi the need to hot-wire the engine.

"We'll take our breaks where we get them," the pilot muttered as he cranked the ignition. White smoke belched from the exhaust and the gears meshed noisily as he worked the clutch and maneuvered the front plow off the ground, giving himself just enough clearance to proceed.

The bulldozer rumbled and groaned as its tanklike treads clawed at the ground, pulling it forward. Grimaldi had seen the damage Umar and Kissinger had inflicted on the second house being used by the JI, and as they joined the Executioner in storming the house, he wrestled with the controls, moving down the unpaved street toward the structure from which the enemy had fired the missile rounds that had brought down the two choppers. Grimaldi could only hope they didn't have a rocket left with his name on it.

NOORDIN ZAILIK WAS DISORIENTED when he regained consciousness. The last thing he remembered was one of the motorcycle officers tackling some demonstrators who'd rushed his car. Now, partly deaf, his face bleeding and his shoulder throbbing with raw pain, he found himself staring up at the backseat of the car. It made no sense. It was only after he'd turned slightly and found himself staring at bits of flaming debris on the road that he realized the car had flipped over. The passenger side of the vehicle was caved in and the windows had all shattered.

A bomb, Zailik thought.

Still dazed, the politician groaned, trying to move. He let out a cry as he shifted his weight onto his injured shoulder. Another shout leapt from his bleeding lips when a hand reached out and grabbed hold of him. He whirled and saw his chauffeur staring at him from a space between his headrest and the collapsed rooftop.

"Don't move, sir."

Zailik could barely hear the man, but he understood what was being said. He stayed put, grimacing, as the chauffeur contorted and slowly wriggled through what was left of the window frame next to him. Once he was out on the road, the driver crawled over and looked in at Zailik.

"Stay put," he told the governor. "I'll get—"

The chauffeur's voice trailed off suddenly and his eyes went blank as blood and gore erupted from his chest and sprayed Zailik. The driver fell to the ground, dead.

Terrified, Zailik stared past the chauffeur's body and caught a glimpse of one of the houses in the partially built development set just off the road. There was movement in one of the upper windows, and when he looked closer, Zailik saw a man taking aim at him through a high-powered rifle. He knew that even if he wasn't injured, there would be no time for him to avoid the sniper's next round....

6

Crouched next to the two spent rocket launchers he'd used to take down the Densus 88 Huey as well as the smaller police chopper, Yorvit Varung propped his elbows on the window-sill of the partially built house and grinned as he peered through the scope of his sniper rife, drawing a bead on Zailik. For Varung, it had already been a glorious day. Besides those in the chopper, he'd also taken out an enemy ground soldier. And now he had a chance to put a bullet through the skull of a despised nemesis who regularly denounced Jemaah Isla-miyah and the notion of clerical rule in Indonesia.

Life was good.

"Take care of him!" snapped Freper Lorten, the sniper's older colleague. He was in a dark mood after witnessing a handful of recruits gunned down and blown to bits on the roadway below. He'd come to know most of the men during their long months of training at a JI encampment outside Calang, and while he understood the need for martyrdom in the name of a greater cause, he was not the sort to gloss over casualties incurred on the battlefield.

"I'll take care of him once I have a clear shot!" Varung retorted without taking his eye off the scope. "If I'd rushed earlier, I wouldn't have brought down the helicopters."

Lorten knew it was pointless to argue with the younger man. Instead, clutching his AK-47, he stared across the road, where surviving members of Densus 88 were caught in a firefight with JI assailants in the foothills behind the tent city. Lorten doubted he could do much to help, so he instead shifted his gaze to the road, looking for a closer target. In front of the overturned car, one of the motorcycle officers was crawling toward the remains of the man who'd nearly thwarted the suicide bomber. The officer was clearly wounded and seemed to pose little threat, but he was still the enemy, so Lorten raised his assault rifle into firing position, ready to finish the man off.

Before either gunman could fire, however, the house shuddered violently, as if struck by an earthquake. The floor beneath them tore loose from the headers and pitched downward with such sudden force that Varung was cast forward, his shot going wild as he plunged headfirst through the open window. The sniper instinctively dropped his rifle and threw his arms out, but there was no time to break his fall. His neck snapped when he struck the ground below, killing him instantly.

Lorten, meanwhile, found himself sliding across the tilted floor toward a gap where the floor had once abutted its supporting wall. He fell through the opening and landed hard on the ground floor below, feetfirst, waves of pain shooting up his legs. Staggering, he fell to his knees, showered with dust and loose plaster, still unsure what had happened. When his AK-47 clattered down to the floor next to him, he grabbed for it, then started to rise.

Hearing the deep rumble of a nearby engine, Lorten spun, spotting the front end of a bulldozer that had just rammed the corner post closest to the road. The bulky earthmover had penetrated the house by several feet, generating enough force to send the second floor crashing down. The vehicle itself was half-buried in rubble, and the man who'd been at the controls had been knocked from the driver's seat.

LORTEN WAS ABOUT TO FIRE at him with his assault rifle when the man suddenly cut loose with his pistol, nailing the sniper with a three-burst killshot to the chest. Lorten fired errantly, then sagged to one side and fell onto a large, splintered section of flooring that had given way.

Jack Grimaldi moved forward and made sure Lorten was dead, then carefully strode through the rubble to the front of the collapsed house, where Yorvit Varung lay dead next to his sniper rifle.

"Two down…" he murmured to himself.

THREE HOUSES AWAY, Mack Bolan had just stormed through the gutted entrance and pressed himself against the entryway wall, M-16 aimed toward the smoky interior. Daud Umar was circling around back and John Kissinger was still out front, closing in on the window through which he'd fired his 40 mm grenade. Bolan could hear the faint crackle of unseen flames where the grenade had done its damage, and if there were any survivors inside, he knew they would be on the move. Thus far, however, there seemed to be no sign of activity.

At the point where the entryway gave way to the wooden framework for what was to be a living room, a swath of sunlight streaked through the thickening haze. As he stared at the light, Bolan glimpsed a moving shadow.

Someone was moving down the hall toward him.

It was too soon for Kissinger or Umar to have entered the house, so the Executioner knew it had to be the enemy. When a long, narrow silhouette emerged from the main shadow, Bolan figured it for a weapon, probably an assault rifle.

Calling out for the man to surrender wasn't an option—Bolan knew he had nothing to gain by betraying his position. Instead, he leveled his carbine at the corner of the entryway and fired an autoburst. The drywall offered little resistance as Bolan's rounds punctured the adjoining walls and took down their intended target.

Bolting forward, Bolan cleared the entryway and whirled

to his right, reaching his victim even before he'd finished collapsing. An AK-47 lay beside him, and in addition to the slugs that had just ripped through his torso, the man had taken shrapnel from Kissinger's grenade. Blood trailed down the hallway to the remains of the room from where the man had been firing moments before. Flames were licking at the shattered doorway, giving off clouds of smoke.

"Okay in there?" Kissinger shouted from his position just outside the front window.

Bolan was about to respond when there was a flurry of motion on the staircase to his immediate left. Another JI warrior was charging down the steps. When Bolan turned toward him, the other man flung himself forward, crashing into the Executioner before he could get a shot off.

The two men fell to the floor, tangled. Bolan's rifle was useless at such close quarters so he cast it aside and grappled with his attacker, ducking a punch aimed for his skull and countering with a fierce swipe of his own. He planted his elbow squarely in the other man's sternum. The terrorist grunted, stunned. The fight went out of him long enough for Bolan to follow up with another blow, this time stiff-arming his assailant in the face, the heel of his palm catching the underside of the other man's nose. Bolan was showered with blood as the man's head snapped back, then fell forward. The blow had killed him.

Bolan pushed the body off of himself.

Kissinger had crawled through the window and made his way to the hall, clutching his M-16/M-203 combo. He coughed in the thickening smoke and helped Bolan to his feet.

"Let's get outta here," he told the Executioner. "This place is a tinderbox."

The men were headed for the front door when they heard an exchange of gunfire behind the house. Detouring through the living room and the framed-out kitchen, the two men saw that the back door was swinging on its hinges. Guns at the ready, they stormed out the doorway.

Daud Umar lay dying on the ground, a bullet wound to his chest. Before the life went out of him, he gestured faintly with his head. Bolan and Kissinger turned and saw the commando's killer had just slipped behind the wheel of a mud-covered mini-Hummer. The vehicle was pointed away from the house, and the assailant crouched low behind the wheel as he gunned the engine and started to pull away. Both Bolan and Kissinger fired, but the Hummer's bulky framework shielded the driver from the blasts.

"I've got him," Bolan called out, already on the run.

With four long strides through rising dust the Executioner was within range of the Hummer. He sprang forward, extending one leg. Grabbing hold of the spare tire mounted to the rear door of the fleeing vehicle, he planted his foot on the raised chrome bumper. He was aboard.

The driver knew it, and the moment he reached the road, he accelerated and yanked the steering wheel, fishtailing the Hummer across the gravel. By then Bolan had brought up his other leg and taken hold of the roof rack, anchoring himself enough to avoid being flung from the vehicle. He knew that as the vehicle picked up speed, it would become increasingly difficult to stay aboard.

The driver drove farther into the housing complex, past half-framed structures and wide, leveled pads where construction had yet to begin. He'd pushed the Hummer up to forty miles an hour and tried swerving back and forth in hopes of shaking Bolan off. When that didn't work, he suddenly slammed on the brakes and turned sharply down a side road, then turned again, heading up onto one of the housing pads. All the while, Bolan held firm, shifting his weight as best he could to counter each maneuver.

Finally, in desperation, the driver bore down on a raised

pile of gravel at the end of the pad. He aimed directly toward the mound, then, at the last second, swerved sharply, striking at an angle. The Hummer pitched sharply to one side, its two right wheels flying off the ground.

Bolan didn't wait to be thrown clear. Sensing what was about to happen, he let go and fell away from the Hummer a split second before it went out of control, striking a fire hydrant and spinning sideways, then rolling, side over side, past the construction pad and down into a culvert.

Battered, Bolan made his way down the incline, drawing a 9 mm Beretta from his web holster. When the driver began to crawl out of the crushed SUV, Bolan stopped and prepared to fire. He held back on the trigger, however, when the man threw his arms up in surrender.

Bolan eyed the man cautiously as he moved closer. Much as he wanted to do away with him for having killed yet another of the Densus 88 commandos, the Executioner knew the man might be more valuable to him alive.

SHELBY FERSTERA and his surviving Densus 88 commandos kept a wary eye on the scattering demonstrators as they got back in their vehicle and made their way around the edge of the tent city. The protestors, in turn, stared back with equal caution, the fight gone out of them.

"I think that bomb took care of the instigators," the Jeep's driver said. "Without JI egging them on, I don't think they're going to cause any more problems."

"I hope you're right, but let's not take any chances," Ferstera murmured from the passenger seat, his assault rifle poised to fire. As they started up a steep dirt road leading to the knoll where the JI snipers had been firing from, the Australian glanced back at the two men riding behind him. "Keep an eye on them," he ordered.

The commandos nodded, never taking their eyes off the dispersing crowd.

The driver downshifted and had to steer his way around a few deep ruts and strewn boulders, but soon he'd cleared the area and reached a level plateau affording him an unobstructed view of the main road below. In the other direction, leading away from the tent city, a meadow of tall grass extended for nearly a quarter mile before giving way to a dense forest.

Just to the right of the Jeep, sprawled on the ground behind the rocks and boulders lining the knoll's edge, they spotted the bodies of three Jemaah Islamiyah sharpshooters that Ferstera and his colleagues had taken out earlier. From the looks of it, they'd all died quickly, dropping close to their firing positions. It was clear, however, that they hadn't been alone.

"Their rifles are missing," Ferstera said. He already had one leg out of the Jeep, and in his next breath he was shouting to his men, "Out!"

As they had earlier on the road, the men sprang quickly from the vehicle. This time, however, they were not immediately fired upon. Still, Ferstera felt certain there was an enemy presence close at hand. He gestured for his men to split up and take cover, then scrambled past one of the fallen snipers and dropped low as he crawled up onto the rocky ledge.

His back to the road, Ferstera peered out across the meadow. The tall, chest-high grass blanketing the flatland undulated slightly in the breeze. Ferstera immediately noticed that there were several telltale creases where the blades had been stepped on or pushed aside.

"You can run but you can't hide," the Aussie whispered.

Once he caught the attention of his men, he gestured toward the meadow, then indicated that he wanted two men to join him up on the promontory. As he waited for them, he turned his attention back to the field, drawing a bead on one of the creases with his M-16. Once he had the trail in his sights, he followed it to where it stopped, halfway across the meadow. He was just able to make out the bulky outline of a man crouched in the grass, moving away from him.

"Shrimp on the barbie," he muttered.

Ferstera held his fire for the moment and shifted his attention to the other creases. There were three of them, one slightly wider than the others. The commando checked the latter trail through his sights and saw two men hunched side-by-side as they made their way across the field, carrying something between them. From that distance, Ferstera couldn't tell for certain what it was.

Ferstera's colleagues were approaching him on the rocks when they all heard the rumble of a helicopter approaching from the west. Ferstera looked up and saw that it was an Apache gunship, most likely dispatched from the army base located five miles down the coast from Banda Aceh. The chopper was headed directly toward them, and he could only hope someone on board would recognize him when he waved to get their attention.

"Take aim at the meadow and be ready to fire!" he told his men.

As the Apache swooped closer, Ferstera pointed toward the field. Whoever was handling surveillance aboard the chopper assessed the situation correctly, and seconds later the gunship thundered past the Densus 88 warriors and put its rotors to good use, flattening the tall grass beneath it.

By the time the chopper was halfway across the meadow, the retreating JI combatants had lost their cover. When they stopped in their tracks and took aim at the Apache, Ferstera's men cut loose with their M-16s. With deadly precision, they dropped the enemy, one by one.

The Apache had taken a couple of ineffective hits to its armored underbelly and remained aloft, fanning down the grass as Ferstera and his men quickly scrambled down from the promontory and went to check on the enemy. There were six men altogether, all slain, two of them on either side of an oblong crate containing an unused rocket launcher as well as the sniper rifles taken from their fallen counterparts.

Once Ferstera signaled that they had things under control, the Apache banked slightly and headed back toward the main road.

"These blokes aren't going anywhere," he told his men. "Gather up their weapons, then we'll help mop up."

By the time the men had brought the confiscated firearms to the Jeep and headed back downhill, a second helicopter had arrived, this one a police chopper similar to the one that had been downed earlier. The road in both directions was choked with an assortment of military vehicles, police cars and ambulances, all headed toward the governor's ill-fated motorcade, sirens wailing, rooftop lights flashing. On the other side of the road, the house Kissinger's grenade had set afire was now fully engulfed in flames, sending a dark smoke cloud into the air. Nearby, the bulldozer Grimaldi had used to take down the other structure was barely visible beneath the debris that had come crashing down on it. The damage had understandably riled the residents of the tent city, but without JI instigators to incite them, it seemed unlikely they would attempt any further show of force, especially in the face of the newly amassed firepower.

Ferstera's men got as close to the overturned car as they could, then piled out of their Jeep and began clearing debris off the road so that the ambulance crews could get to Zailik. Muhtar Yeilam had crawled around to the side of the car and stationed himself next to the flattened section where the governor remained trapped. Blood was pooling beneath his wounded leg, and when he looked at the man, Ferstera could tell that the motorcycle officer was in shock. The man's eyes were red and it was clear that he'd been weeping.

"It's over, mate," Ferstera told him as EMTs moved in with kits and stretchers. "You can relax."

"My brother," Muhtar whispered hoarsely, his voice filled with anguish.

The paramedics asked Ferstera to give them more room, so he moved away, crossing to the entranceway to the housing project. The big American was there, crouched before a prisoner, who sat with his hands over his head, back pressed against the brickwork supporting the main gate. The other two Americans stood on either side of him, their assault rifles aimed at the prisoner. Ferstera assumed the man was being interrogated.

"I hope you've wrung something out of this bastard," he told Bolan as he joined them.

"A little," Bolan responded. "He says they worked in teams, mostly three or four men apiece. They were given their assignments and pretty much kept in the dark about everything else."

"That's the way they work, all right," Ferstera said. "Keeps them from being able to spill too much if they get taken alive."

"Case in point," Grimaldi said.

"We got something else, too," Bolan said. "The reason they knew Zailik was coming this way to the airport instead of taking the main road."

"Mole?" Ferstera guessed.

Bolan nodded. "A woman who worked in Zailik's office…"

Ti Vohn knew she'd been caught when the governor started leaving messages on her cell phone. By then she'd already left work early and returned to her apartment, a modest three-room unit in a decades-old complex that had been spared the tsunami's wrath. Wary that Zailik may have spread word of her duplicity, she was quickly gathering a few necessities, ready to go into hiding. She didn't have a plan yet, but if the assassination succeeded, she knew that she would be able to go to her lover, Buowono, the man she'd called earlier to report the governor's decision to take the back road to the airport. Buowono—who went by that name alone—was the Jemaah Islamiyah team leader in Banda Aceh, the man who'd masterminded the plot. An expert marksman, Buowono's plan had been to head up a sniper team posted in the hills behind the tent city Zailik would be passing, far removed from the suicide team that would attempt to set a bomb off once they got near the governor's motorcade. He'd assured Vohn he would call her once the assassination had been carried out so that they could arrange a rendezvous to celebrate.

Once she'd stuffed her purse with as much as it could hold, Vohn checked her watch for the twelfth time in the past ten minutes. The attack should have been carried out by now, and yet Buowono hadn't called. She tried to calm herself and ignore her building anxiety. It wasn't working.

Finally, she broke down and moved to the television. She'd put off turning it on, fearing what she would see. The moment the screen flickered to life, her apprehensions were quickly confirmed. Regular programming had been preempted in favor of live coverage of the bloodbath that had just taken place on the outskirts of Banda Aceh. Weak in the knees, the secretary slowly sat down on the edge of her coffee table and watched with numb wonder as field reporters spelled out what happened. In quick succession, she learned that Zailik had been wounded during the attack on his motorcade and was en route to a nearby hospital. There had been extensive casualties, including a member of Zailik's police escort and those killed in two downed helicopters, one containing a squad of Densus 88 commandos. The attack was being blamed on Jemaah Islamiyah. The number of assailants had not yet been confirmed, but according to reports, only one member of JI had been taken into custody alive.

The last bit of news had been accompanied by footage of several men standing alongside a man seated on the dirt near the gateway to the unfinished housing complex located just off the road where the attack had taken place. The man wasn't Buowono.

A muted whimper escaped from Ti Vohn's lips as she leaned forward and turned off the television. Her gaze went to her cell phone. She tried to convince herself there was still a chance Buowono had gotten away and would call once he'd reached safety. It was a fleeting notion, and as quickly as it had occurred to her, she knew it was a lie. Buowono was dead. Gone. And gone with him was her assurance of protection, not only from the authorities, but also the even greater threat posed by the man she had alienated herself from the moment she'd taken to Buowono's bed—

Agmed Hasem.

The Makassar field leader had sworn that Ti Vohn would live to regret spurning him for Buowono, and during the years she had spent under Hasem's possessive control she knew the savage brutality he was capable of. But so long as Buowono was alive, she also knew that Hasem dared not make good on his threat, as Buowono ranked above him in the JI pecking order and any move against him would be seen within the ranks as an act of sedition. Now, if Buowono indeed had been killed, there was nothing to stop Hasem from coming after her.

The woman's shock over the turn of events gave way to panic. Grabbing the cell phone and her purse, she bolted for the door and threw it open, ready to flee into the night.

She didn't get far.

She was heading out of the apartment complex when she froze in her tracks. Standing at the foot of the stairs, staring up at her, was a wiry, ferret-eyed Indonesian whose receding hairline made him look much older than his thirty years. She knew the man, but he was the last person she would have expected to find at her doorstep.

"I just saw the news," he told her. "I figured you could use my help."

7

Gapang Bay, Weh Island, Indonesia

"Her name is Ti Vohn," explained Provincial Intelligence Director Sinso Dujara. "She's the governor's personal secretary. I was actually on the phone with her right after Zailik decided he was going to take the back way to the airport."

Dujara was standing on the balcony of the beachfront condo disgraced former ambassador Carl Ryan had rented under an assumed identity shortly after his return to Indonesia. Ryan stood with Dujara and Zailik's chief political rival, GAM gubernatorial candidate Anhi Hasbrok. The men had just finished the soup Ryan had made from the gutted hawksbill turtle he'd killed earlier out in the bay. They were just a stone's throw from the water, which stretched out before them, about to swallow the setting sun.

It was Dujara who was supposed to have witnessed Hasbrok's receipt of the nonexistent weapons Rhan Leibyla had gone to his death expecting to retrieve from the jungle wilderness of Gunung Leuser National Park two days earlier. Dujara had conspired with Hasbrok to arrange the convoluted ambushes that had made Leibyla's death appear to have been ordered by Zailik. And because he headed up the investigation into the killings, Dujara was confident that Zailik would never learn the truth, either about his duplicity or the fact that Leibyla had been murdered to keep secret GAM's covert maintenance of its militia in direct violation of the organization's disarmament agreement following the 2004 tsunami. The plan, of course, had been for the jungle killings to shed a bad light on Zailik and increase the chances that the governorship would go to Hasbrok, who had promised Dujara a more prominent—and lucrative—position in the new administration in exchange for betraying the man who'd appointed him to head up the region's intelligence operations. But now, in the wake of a failed assassination attempt, both Dujara and Hasbrok were concerned that public sentiment would sway in Zailik's favor. They, along with Ryan, were attempting to come to grips with the unexpected turn of events.

"So, after speaking to you she called her contacts with Jemaah Islamiyah to arrange the attack," Hasbrok said, piecing together the information Dujara had just passed along after speaking by phone with the Banda Aceh police chief and the military commander who'd overseen mop-up operations at the battle site.

"It might have been before," Dujara conceded. He was a short, lean man with a taste for fine suits and hand-rolled Havana cigars, one of which he trimmed with a special clipper before lighting up and adding to the smoky haze that already hung over the balcony thanks to Hasbrok's cheaper cigarillos. "At this point it's really not all that important."

To Carl Ryan, none of this was important, as it had little to do with the agenda he'd plotted out during his months in prison back in America. He hadn't been opposed to the ambushes Hasbrok had orchestrated earlier because if Rhan Leibyla had blown the whistle on GAM's covert militia, it could well have come out that Ryan, while still U.S. ambassador, knew about Hasbrok's troops yet turned a blind eye to their existence. In exchange, he'd negotiated for the right to have them placed at his disposal should circumstances dictate. Ryan had gone to prison before calling in the marker, but he planned to make use of the goon squad in carrying out his mission. Now, however, with JI rattling its sabers in the wake of those ambushes, he was concerned the U.S. government would sense anarchy in the wings and tighten security at its installations throughout Indonesia. It was the last thing Ryan wanted to have to take into consideration.

"You mentioned that a chopper full of Densus 88 commandos was destroyed in the attack," Ryan said to Dujara.

The intelligence director nodded, wreathing the air before him with a smoke circle. "My guess is they were as much a target as Zailik, given all the problems they've been causing JI the past few years."

"You're probably right," Ryan conceded before getting to the matter that concerned him foremost. "You also said something about Densus not being alone when they went to assist the motorcade."

"Correct," Dujara said. "They had a couple extra men with them. Americans flown in from the States. As it turned out, they all survived the attack."

Ryan frowned. It wasn't adding up for him.

"These Americans," he said. "They obviously didn't know anything about a planned attack, so they must've been flown in for another reason."

"Could be," Dujara replied. "I wasn't apprised of their mission."

"Do you know who they're with?" Ryan asked. "CIA? Delta Force?"

Dujara shrugged. There was a trace of annoyance in the tight-lipped smile he offered Ryan. "You know how you Americans are about keeping a tight lid on things when it comes to your covert operations. You'd think I'd be let in to the loop given that this is supposed to be my turf. But, no, they've chosen to keep me in the dark. For all I know, these men could be from your Mafia or the Internal Revenue Service."

Hasbrok let out a hearty laugh, but Ryan was in no mood for Dujara's levity. He suspected that the Americans dispatched to Banda Aceh had come specifically to look for him. Maybe Dujara wasn't concerned about finding out who they were, but Ryan sure as hell was. He just had to figure out the best way to go about it.

Stony Man Farm, Virginia

HAL BROGNOLA HAD RETURNED from his White House briefing and filled in Barbara Price on the latest developments in Indonesia.

Governor Zailik had sustained a broken collarbone and mild concussion along with minor facial lacerations in the attack on his motorcade. He was expected to remain hospitalized for observation for at least another day before being released. He'd already put out a press statement denouncing Jemaah Islamiyah, and the terrorist sect had countered with a Web site posting praising their fallen comrades and vowing to continue their fight against those who opposed their dream of turning Indonesia into an Islamic state. Indonesia's president had weighed in on the matter, echoing Zailik's message and adding another million dollars to the bounty on the heads of JI's leadership, including Agmed Hasem.

"Sounds like things are ratcheting up," Price commented upon hearing the news.

Brognola nodded. "JI's posting made reference to Americans being involved in the response to their attack, so we've got the usual Great Satan rhetoric to deal with on top of everything else."

"No surprise there," Price said.

"True," Brognola replied. "Of course, now we have to watch our backs even more over there. The president's putting the embassy in lockdown and sending backup security to the consulates."

"Sounds like our little hunt for Carl Ryan is slipping onto the back burner," Price said.

"I'm not so sure about that," Brognola confided. "When you figure all this mayhem coincides with his suspected return to the country, we should consider that he's involved somehow. We need to keep him on our radar."

"To do that, we need to get him on our radar first, though, right?"

Brognola nodded. "I talked to Bear," he said. "They're making progress on that end."

They headed to the computer room, where Aaron Kurtzman was hard at work at his computer. At separate work stations behind him, two other members of his cybernetic crew were busy as well. Carmen Delahunt, a sharp-tongued redhead who'd joined Stony Man after a stint with the FBI, was hunched over her keyboard, eyes glued to her monitor, so caught up in her work she hadn't seen Brognola and Price enter. At the station next to her, Akira Tokaido was adjusting his iPod headset as he waited for a computer printout to finish spilling from the feeder perched on his mainframe.

Brognola waited until he had Tokaido's attention, then gestured for the Japanese-American to nix his music for the time being.

"Sorry," Tokaido said. "Just needed a quick Audioslave fix."

"I won't even ask what that means," Brognola said. "Bear said you were working on something to help us track down Ryan."

"Coming right up," Tokaido said. As he reached for the printout that had just come out of the feeder, he explained, "I glommed on to a note from Ryan's parole officer saying how the guy'd lost a ton of weight while he was in the pen. My guess is he's not quite as fat in the face as he was in the photos we've been sending out."

"You ran him through Identi-Kit?" Price asked.

"Yep," Tokaido said, handing Brognola the printout. "Voila."

There were five images on the sheet, all computer-altered mugshots depicting the former ambassador as much thinner than in his booking photo or other shots on file in the Stony Man database. Tokaido had also factored in other possible changes Ryan might have made to his appearance in hopes of avoiding detection once he fled the country. One shot had Ryan sporting a blond wig and full beard, while another went to the opposite extreme, showing Ryan as bald and clean-shaven. The other shots covered variations in between.

"Nice work," Brognola said. "You want to feed these into the database and send them out?"

"Will do," Tokaido said. "I'll hit the airports within a hundred-mile radius of DC and cast a little wider net along the Pacific Rim."

"Good," Brognola said.

Tokaido cranked up his music once again as Brognola and Price headed to Kurtzman's workstation.

"It makes sense that Ryan would try a makeover," Price said.

Kurtzman agreed. "It would also explain why there haven't been any sightings of him."

"Odds are he's forged a new ID, too," Brognola said.

"Carmen's on it," Kurtzman responded quickly. "The black market for that stuff goes wider than what we've got on file, though, so that's going to be a long shot."

"Understood," Brognola said. "What else are we working on?"

"This has less to do with Ryan than JI," Kurtzman said, "but we're making some headway on this woman who tried to feed Zailik to the sharks."

"Ti Vohn," Price said.

"Well, that's one of her aliases," Kurtzman replied. He worked his cursor and called up a file on Zailik's personal secretary. "She came out of a steno pool in Medan with top-notch recommendations and a clean record, but we dug a little deeper and found she had another life before that. She was enrolled at Jakarta U under another name, majoring in political science and religious studies. She mixed in with some fringe radical groups, including a couple that doubled as recruiting centers for Jemaah Islamiyah."

"They liked what they saw and groomed her as a mole," Brognola surmised.

"Looks that way," Kurtzman said, eyeing the data on the monitor. "She started out with a JI shell company in Sulawesi until she had her secretarial chops down, then changed her name and somehow wrangled her way to a regency office in Sumatra. Two years there, another three in Medan, then she wound up with Zailik."

"That's a lot of grooming," Price said.

"A lot of connections, too," Brognola added. "Sounds like she'd be worth getting into an interrogation room."

"Yeah, if we can find her," Kurtzman said. "By the time news broke about the motorcade attack, she was AWOL from the gov's office. CIA checked her home address but she'd already been there and given the place a clean sweep before disappearing."

"You ask me," Brognola said, "it's not just us she's running from. Now that Zailik's outed her, she's a liability to JI. They're probably after her, too."

"If that's the case," Price said, "She better hope we get to her before they do…"

8

Sulawesi, Indonesia

"You're sure?" Agmed Hasem asked Guikin Daeng, as he stared over his subordinate's shoulder at the laptop computer set up in the corner of the JI field leader's Quonset hut.

"I've told you a hundred times," Daeng snapped, taking his eyes off the blog site on which Jemaah Islamiyah had claimed responsibility for the assassination attempt on Governor Zailik. "The postings are anonymous. There's no way they can be traced directly to you, much less this computer."

Hasem scowled, bristling at Daeng's insolence. There were times, like this, when he wished he'd taken the time to learn about computers instead of decrying them as tools of Western decadence. As it was, he'd come to learn that concessions needed to be made to modern technology and, as such, he'd reluctantly bestowed responsibility for his field team's computer operations on Daeng, the only man he knew who was qualified and trustworthy enough to handle the job. That Daeng knew he'd become indispensable had clearly gone to the man's head, giving him a haughty air Hasem would never tolerate from anyone else under his command.

"What about Ti Vohn?" Hasem asked, changing the subject. "Has anyone been in touch with her?"

"Since the attack? No," Daeng replied.

"And the stakeout at her place?"

"It was called off," Daeng said.

"Called off? Why?"

"The place was being searched by some Americans when our people showed up," Daeng explained. "They thought there might be backup teams on the lookout, so they took off."

"Then we have no way of knowing if she showed up and was taken into custody," Hasem said, his temper rising.

The JI recruiter had been obsessed with tracking down his former lover ever since he'd received an unexpected call the previous day from a contact in Banda Aceh fishing for some kind of reward if he brought Ti Vohn to Hasem. When Hasem had balked, the other man, a street hustler named Dihb Wilki, had hung up on him, forcing Hasem to make a series of frantic calls to the few remaining Banda Aceh operatives he could trust, hoping they would be able to get their hands on the woman before Wilki.

"They should have stayed there!" Hasem ranted. "What else are they doing to try to find her?!"

"They didn't say," Daeng said. "And if you ask me, they were right to leave. You would have done the same thing."

Hasem grabbed Daeng by the collar, pulling him from his chair with so much force the younger man's legs slammed against the underside of the rickety table. The computer skimmed across the tabletop and caromed off the wall, its power cord snapping free as it toppled with a dull thud into an opened cardboard box filled with trash.

"Now look what you did!" Hasem shouted, shaking Daeng.

"It was your fault!" Daeng scoffed.

The younger man tried to free himself but Hasem had tightened his grip on the collar and was shaking him even harder, keeping him off balance. When Daeng started to fall, Hasem kicked his shin and pushed him hard to one side, sending him tumbling across the floor. Daeng crashed hard into the curved, metallic wall and the entire hut shook, raining flecks of rust down into the musty enclosure. He was getting up when Hasem strode forward and kicked him again, this time in the stomach. Daeng doubled over and cried out in pain. By the time he looked back up at his attacker, Hasem had pulled a Walther pistol from his waistband.

"Who are you to offer unsolicited advice?" Hasem shouted, aiming the gun at Daeng's forehead. "Who are you to tell me what I would do?"

Daeng stared at his superior and forced himself to remain calm. It wasn't the first time he'd had to endure one of Hasem's violent outbursts. True, the field leader had never gone so far as to pull a gun on him before, but in every other respect Daeng felt the situation was the same as the others. He knew all he had to do was let Hasem vent and get the frustration out of his system and in a few minutes the tantrum would pass. Hasem would offer a backhanded apology and go out of his way to make things right between them again. Daeng found Hasem's predictability almost comical and figured it would one day prove the leader's undoing. In the meantime, he would play along, pricking what was left of the other man's conscience until the guilt kicked in and defused his temper.

"I thought you valued my opinion," Daeng responded quietly, staring past the gun's barrel into Hasem's eyes. "You're always saying how important it is not to surround yourself with nothing but yes-men and—"

"You didn't answer my question," Hasem interrupted. "Who are you to tell me what I would do?"

"Your friend?" Daeng answered. "A friend who has known you longer than anyone else at this entire camp."

"You're not a friend, you're an opportunist!" Hasem countered. "You saw the need for a computer expert here and you've abused it ever since."

"I see," Daeng said, stung by the accusation. Without thinking, he blurted out a response. "And if I point out that we'll probably need a new computer now to replace the one you just ruined, that somehow makes me an opportu—"

A shot rang out inside the hut and silenced Daeng in mid-sentence, splattering his brains on the wall behind him. Toppling to one side, he fell hard against the cardboard box, knocking it over. The laptop slid onto the floor along with a pile of trash.

Hasem slowly lowered his gun, staring down at the man he'd just executed. He spat at Daeng, filled with contempt.

"I'll replace you along with the computer," he said calmly.

Banda Aceh

MACK BOLAN AND Shelby Ferstera emerged from Governor Zailik's hospital room, no closer to knowing the whereabouts of his personal secretary than when they'd gone in to question him.

"Would've been nice if he'd been shagging her on the side, eh?" Ferstera opined as they headed down the hall. "Then we'd at least have a love nest to check out."

"We'll have to find a lead somewhere else," Bolan said.

There was a vending machine halfway down the corridor. They bought coffee and sandwiches, then sat in the corner of a large waiting area. There were only a few other people in the room, all busy with magazines or watching the wall-mounted television, which was tuned to continuing coverage of the attack on Governor Zailik. Ferstera sipped his coffee, then voiced the concern that had been gnawing at him since the moment he'd seen the Huey go down with the bulk of his Densus 88 crew onboard.

"I should've smelled a trap," he said glumly. "The whole bloody thing smacked of an ambush."

"No sense going there," Bolan told him.

"Maybe so," Ferstera said. "Like they say, hindsight's a bitch."

"No luck tracking down the informant who told you JI was planning something?" Bolan asked.

Ferstera shook his head.

"The bastard had been on the up-and-up for us from day one," Ferstera recounted. He took a bite from his sandwich then continued. "We knocked out a pair of sleeper cells in Lamno and Calang based on what he passed along to us."

"It could be he's still reliable," Bolan offered. "After all, he was on the mark as far as JI going after the motorcade."

"If he's clean, we would have heard back from him by now."

"Maybe not," Bolan suggested. "Considering the way things turned out, maybe he's afraid to check in because he thinks you blame him."

"Well, he's right. You may have a point, though." Ferstera finished his sandwich, then wiped his fingers on his pantlegs.

Something occurred to Bolan and he played devil's advocate. "On the other hand, if he's on the level, it seems like he would've known about the secretary and let you know she was a mole."

The Densus 88 commando mulled that over as he went back to his coffee. By the time he'd drained the cup, there was a faint gleam in his eye and Bolan sensed that he'd just triggered the lead they were looking for.

"Blimey!" Ferstera said. "It's been right there in front of my face all along!"

"You think Vohn might have gone on the run with your informant," Bolan guessed.

"Nail on the head, mate," Ferstera replied. "And maybe Zailik doesn't know squat about where Vohn liked to hang out when she punched off work, but I know Wilki's moves like the back of my bleedin' hand!"

DIHB WILKI FUMBLED through his pockets as he exited a cab that had pulled to the curb across the street from Banda Aceh's

West Shore Marina. As he leaned back in to pay the fare, Ti
Vohn wriggled past him onto the sidewalk. Purse in hand,
wearing sunglasses, and with her hair tucked under a large
straw hat, she'd made a feeble attempt at a disguise. But, given
their surroundings, the precaution hardly seemed necessary.

This part of the city had been hit the hardest by the 2004
tsunami and had thus far been the slowest to rebound in its
aftermath. Most of the hotels and tourist haunts were boarded
up, and there were only a handful of vessels moored out on
the water, as most boating enthusiasts had chosen to make use
of rebuilt marinas on the other side of the city.

"It's like a ghost town," Vohn remarked, taking in the bleak
desolation around her.

"Just the way we want it," the street hustler told her. "The
fewer witnesses around, the better."

"You're probably right."

"Of course I'm right," Wilki told her as the taxi pulled
away. "I keep telling you not to worry. I'll take care of you.
We're going to be okay."

Vohn was skeptical but managed a faint smile.

For Wilki, it was the same smile that had stirred up lust the
moment he'd first crossed paths with the woman shortly after
her arrival in Banda Aceh. Five months earlier, he'd chanced
upon Ti Vohn at a food stand near the governor's residence.
At the time, he'd had no idea that she was, like him, secretly
in collusion with Jemaah Islamiyah. She'd been equally in the
dark about his convoluted dealings with JI, Densus 88 and any
local police officials willing to pay him for useful information he came across while working the streets. He'd approached her, one stranger to another, and had asked her out,
only to be politely rebuffed. Undaunted, over the next few
weeks he'd continued to haunt the same food stand during her
lunch hour, content to exchange pleasantries and build a
rapport before trying to make another move on her.

During one such moment Vohn had been approached by one of the same JI intermediaries Wilki dealt with, and once it came out that they were kindred spirits, Wilki had hoped their common bond would bring them closer. Vohn had felt just the opposite, telling Wilki it was too risky for them to be seen together and confessing that she wasn't attracted to him anyway. Wilki had been gracious in the face of rejection and remained cordial with Vohn the several times they'd found themselves in the same room with JI teams plotting a retaliatory strike against both Zailik and Densus 88.

It was during one of these meetings that Wilki had noticed the number of furtive, telling glances between Vohn and Buowono, the team's leader. After the meeting, he'd taken Vohn aside and told her he now realized she had turned down his advances because she was Buowono's lover. Ti Vohn had denied it, but the way she'd been taken aback had, for Wilki, confirmed his suspicions. Intrigued, he'd looked deeper into her past, and in speaking to other JI functionaries, he'd learned the woman had once been the bedmate of Agmed Hasem, the Makassar Madman, a field leader with whom Wilki had a passing acquaintance.

A call to Hasem put into motion the plan that placed Wilki at Vohn's apartment the previous night, ready to exploit her vulnerability following Buowono's death in the assassination attempt on Zailik. He'd told her he was now on the run as well and had convinced her he knew a way they could both avoid being tracked down. The couple had spent the night three miles from town, hiding out at a remote hunting cabin owned by one of Wilki's underworld contacts. Now they were prepared to resume their flight.

As they crossed the deserted street, Wilki pointed to a midsized cabin cruiser moored in one of the slips. "That's it," he said. "Fastest boat its size you're going to find."

The boat had been listed for sale on a local Web site Wilki

had searched while they had breakfast at an Internet café near the marina. The cruiser was equipped with all the features Wilki was looking for, and the fact that the owner kept the boat at West Shore instead of one of the busier marinas had assured him he'd found their ticket out of Banda Aceh.

The boat's owner, a retired commercial fisherman in his early sixties, stood by himself out on the docks, thirty yards from a bait-and-tackle shop that doubled as the marina office. An old scooter with a dented fender was parked next to the shanty, but Wilki figured the owner had most likely driven to the docks in the battered car parked on a dirt strip just off the road. There were no other cars in the makeshift lot. This would be easy, Wilki figured.

"Just remember to turn on the charm and keep him distracted," he advised Vohn once they'd reached the docks.

"The way I did with the governor?" Vohn said, a trace of annoyance in her voice. "I think I know how to do that."

Wilki was put off by the woman's sudden change of mood, but there was nothing to be gained by calling her on it.

"Of course," he told her.

Things went as planned when Wilki met the fisherman, introducing Vohn as a cousin who'd come to visit after her marriage breakup. The older man seemed intrigued by the idea that a woman as attractive as Vohn might be available and on the rebound. Vohn played along, offering her best smile and maintaining eye contact with the man so that he would pay more attention to her than Wilki as they went to look the boat over. When Wilki asked the capacity of the fuel tanks, the owner told him, adding, "I just filled them both yesterday."

Wilki nodded but did his best to look noncommittal. Inside, though, he was more than pleased. The owner didn't realize it, but he'd just signed his death warrant.

Once they'd looked over the exterior, the owner led Wilki and Vohn aboard to check out the rest of the boat. Eager to keep

the man at ease and convinced he was truly an interested buyer,
Wilki asked a few innocuous questions about the maintenance
work that had been done and how the boat held up when the
sea was choppy. He acted satisfied with the answers, and as
they made their way inside the main cabin, Wilki asked how
firm the asking price was. As expected, there was some leeway.

"I'll show you the controls and the sleeping quarters, then
we can discuss specifics," the owner said.

"Specifics about the sleeping quarters?" Vohn asked,
smiling at the man, one eyebrow raised suggestively.

"Well, I suppose we can discuss anything you'd like," the
owner countered, taking the bait.

"Before we do that," Wilki interjected, gesturing at the
ship's washroom, "could I use the facilities?"

"Help yourself," the man chuckled. "I'll keep your
cousin company."

Wilki excused himself and closed the door behind him. He
reached into his back pocket, withdrawing a three-foot length
of thin electrical cable. He coiled each end of the cable around
his hands, then pulled it taut, testing the cord's strength.

Wilki waited a few moments, listening to Vohn and the
owner share a laugh over something she'd just said. Then, as
quietly as possible, he reached out and slowly turned the door
handle. When Vohn let out a sudden sneeze, Wilki knew that
she'd positioned the owner where he wanted him. He waited
for a second sneeze, using it to mask the sound of the door
latch clicking open.

When Wilki emerged from the lavatory, the boat's owner
was standing only a few feet away, his back turned, preoccupied with Vohn. Wilki raised his arms and quickly swung the
makeshift garrote over the other man's head, then lowered it
to his neck and pulled tight.

The owner let out a gasp and reeled backward. Wilki leaned
forward and crossed his hands, twisting the cable tighter

around the man's neck. The man flailed his arms as his face turned crimson. He reached up, clawing at the cord. Wilki tugged harder and brought his hands up slightly, giving his victim nothing to grab. It only took a few seconds before the man went limp.

Wilki lowered the body to the cabin floor, then unwound the cable from his hands and quickly rifled through the dead man's pockets, coming up with a wallet as well as the keys to the boat's ignition. The wallet was thick with currency.

"Our lucky day," Wilki said, smiling up at Vohn, who stared at the dead man with a look of both horror and relief. "Not only do we have a boat, but our friend here has given us a little traveling money…."

9

Gapang, Weh Island, Indonesia

Anhi Hasbrok stepped away from the podium in the banquet room at the prestigious Bay Retreat Hotel, ignoring the shouted pleas of reporters clamoring for a question-and-answer period. It was bad enough he'd had to bow to political expediency and go on the record wishing Governor Zailik a quick recovery from the injuries he'd sustained in the motorcade attack. There was no way he was about to stand around and give Zailik any more sympathy votes by appearing overeager to take advantage of the situation and forge ahead with his campaign while the governor was still laid up in the hospital. It would have been fine with him if the bastard had died.

Habrok's security entourage quickly surrounded him once he left the banquet room and strode purposefully from the hotel. There was a crowd of reporters, photographers and cameramen waiting outside for him.

"I have no further comment," he told them, hoping to preempt any more badgering. Questions were shouted as he headed for his car. He was able to tune out all but one.

"What do you say to the rumors that JI tried to assassinate the governor on your behalf in retaliation for the murder of those GAM workers found in the jungle the other day?"

Hasbrok whirled and glared angrily at the press.

"Who said that?" he demanded.

A rakish-looking reporter in a designer suit and lightly tinted glasses stepped forward, a half smirk creasing his face as he eyed Hasbrok. Raj Mestra was Indonesia's most celebrated muckraker. Before Hasbrok could respond, Mestra quickly followed up his own question.

"It's said that Jemaah Islamiyah prefers you over Zailik because of your track record as a military separatist. They feel you're something of a brother-in-arms, so to speak."

"Feel free to hide behind your journalistic license and spread all the lies you want," Hasbrok responded defiantly. "But you know as well as I do that JI wants a clerical state. Their candidate of choice is Nyak Lamm."

"Nyak Lamm has no chance of winning the election," Mestra countered. "They know that. They would prefer you over Governor Zailik."

"I don't want their support," Hasbrok shot back. "And if you'd listened to my speech instead of baiting your hook to get a rise out of me, you'd have heard me denounce the attack on the governor as well as any and all attempts by Jemaah Islamiyah to subvert the political process."

"Would it be safe to say, then, that you regret your own attempts to subvert the political process while carrying out terrorist acts when you headed up the militia for Gerakan Aceh Merdeka?"

Hasbrok stared at Mestra with disgust. He knew it had been a mistake to let Mestra lure him into an exchange, and he could only hope that some of the other news units would edit their sound bites in a way that showed the muckraker for the unscrupulous ratings monger that he was. Rather than prolong their confrontation and allow Mestra to toss out more innuendo, Hasbrok turned his back on the reporter and returned to his car. One of his aides had already opened the door for him. He got in, and once the door was closed, he cursed himself.

"Idiot!" he ranted, smacking the back of the seat directly in front of him. "You played right into his hand!"

The former GAM strongman continued to fume as he was driven from the hotel and taken on a circuitous route along the back roads of Gapang, shaking off any news teams that might have tried to follow him. In the aftermath of the jungle killings, it had looked as if he were about to pull ahead of Zailik in the polls once and for all. But, less than twenty-four hours later, the pendulum had already swung the other way. And if Mestra somehow managed to resurrect the issue of his military past and succeeded in getting the public to draw unfavorable parallels between GAM and Jemaah Islamiyah, his candidacy would likely be dead in the water.

Hasbrok's brooding was interrupted by the bleat of his cell phone. It was Intelligence Director Dujara, who'd returned to the mainland following their meeting with Carl Ryan the night before.

"Nice job whittling that Mestra down to size," Dujara said.

"Are you being sarcastic?" Hasbrok retorted.

"Hardly," Dujara said. "The way it looked from here, you put that sideshow barker in his place."

Hasbrok was surprised. Had he really come off better than he'd thought?

"That's not why I'm calling," Dujara said. "I may have something for you. It has something to do with the Americans who were involved in that whole business with Zailik's motorcade."

"What about them?"

"I'm still not sure what agency they're with, but they just met with Police Chief Alkihn here in Banda," Dujara reported. "They were getting the names of some street thugs who have dealings with an informant who's on the payroll for both the cops and Densus 88. The informant's name is Dihb Wilki. Apparently he's the one who tipped Densus off that JI was going to attack the motorcade. He's turned up missing and they think he's with Zailik's secretary."

"The one Zailik says betrayed him?" Hasbrok asked.

"Correct," Dujara replied. "The feeling is that both she and Wilki owe their first allegiance to JI. They probably know their cover's been blown, which means they're either on the run or have gone into hiding. The Americans are hoping one of Wilki's contacts will be able to tell them which."

"And why does this concern me?" Hasbrok asked.

"For starters, you can pass along the information to your friend Ryan so he'll keep thinking we're eager to jump through hoops for him," Dujara told him.

"There is that," Hasbrok conceded.

Neither he nor Dujara knew exactly how many millions of dollars in tsunami funds Ryan had stashed away before his arrest, but both men knew it was worth stringing the former ambassador along in hopes of somehow getting their hands on it. And thus far Ryan clearly had no idea that he was being played as surely as one of the big game fish Hasbrok was fond of going after in Gapang Bay.

"The other reason is political," Dujara continued. "If you can beat the Americans to Wilki and Vohn, you can take credit for taking down the spies who made it possible for Jemaah Islamiyah to have a crack at the governor. You'll steal back his sympathy vote and squelch any notions Mestra is fostering about you being a JI sympathizer."

Dujara was making perfect sense, and Hasbrok's spirits rose briefly, only to be tempered by a logistical stumbling block.

"There's one problem," Hasbrok said. "I supposedly don't have a militia at my disposal. If I use my men to go after Wilki and Vohn, Mestra will put two and two together and the whole thing will backfire."

"That is a problem," Dujara admitted. "But I'm sure you'll think of something."

CARL RYAN SURFACED from the azure depths of Gapang Bay and swam to the small, unattended rental boat he'd left anchored a hundred yards offshore. He'd returned empty-handed save for the tools he'd brought to free the waterproof container hidden beneath the coral shelf. He'd returned to the hiding place and had gone so far as to start unfastening one of the bars shielding the container, but at the last minute he'd changed his mind and given up the task. His paranoia had gotten the better of him, and he decided it was too risky to retrieve the container if there was a chance the Americans aligned with Densus 88 had come to Banda Aceh specifically to seek him out. Until that matter was resolved, the container would have to wait.

Once Ryan shed his scuba gear and started up the boat, he circled around and headed back toward shore, making a point to steer wide of several other diving teams whose boats were anchored in the shallow water. There was a private dock for renters at his beachside condominium complex, and once he'd moored the craft, Ryan walked to his unit to change before his scheduled meeting with Hasbrok.

It was while shaving in the shower, dragging a disposable razor across the day-old stubble on his neck, that Ryan was struck by a flash of inspiration. He stared at the razor, mental gears racing. He'd figured out a way to put an end to any manhunt the Americans might have initiated against him.

ANHI HASBROK may have just denounced Jemaah Islamiyah and taken offense at the suggestion that his involvement with the Free Aceh Movement mirrored that of those running the terrorist sect, but, in truth, the gubernatorial candidate had borrowed a page from the JI playbook when he'd agreed to disband GAM's military arm in exchange for political recognition following the 2004 tsunami. Yes, he'd weeded out a few soldiers for appearances' sake, but instead of dismantling his

entire armed forces, he'd merely splintered them into smaller
units and dispersed them, like terrorist sleeper cells, throughout the islands. He'd periodically replenished his campaign
coffers by brokering out troops as mercenaries or goon squads
to anyone willing to put up the right amount of money, and—
as in the case of the ambush killings in Gunung Leuser—there
were times when he'd used the men for his own purposes. But,
for the most part, the GAM commandos had kept a low
profile, training intermittently at remote facilities near the
towns and villages where, under assumed names, they led
somewhat normal lives. Each group had its own commander,
and, at regular intervals, Hasbrok summoned these leaders
together for strategy sessions…and to assure himself that
he'd retained their loyalty.

Hasbrok had scheduled one such conference at the hide-
away being used by his commandos on Weh Island, and now,
two hours after leaving his press conference at the Bay Retreat
Hotel, he was waiting for the arrival of a team leader from Java
so that he could get the meeting underway. The camp, a one-
time Christian spiritual retreat, was located in the middle of
the island near the base of a slumbering volcano whose
periodic rumblings and sulfuric belchings had chased off the
pilgrims and made it an unlikely tourist destination. A canopy
of treetops shrouded the camp from aerial view and, to a
degree, helped filter out any stench wafting down from the
higher elevations.

While the other leaders huddled around one of the mess
tables set near the converted chapel that now served as a
barracks, Hasbrok had taken aside Hoa Mursneh, the scar-
faced team leader who'd carried out the massacres in Gunung
Leuser. The retreat was Mursneh's base of operations, and his
men were at the camp as well, using the volcano's steep slope
for uphill runs as part of their daily fitness regimen.

"Again, my compliments on a job well done," Hasbrok

told his underling, handing him an envelope stuffed with currency. "To have carried it out was tricky enough. Using crocodiles to get rid of some evidence…that was a brilliant improvisation."

"It'll be brilliant if they don't manage to x-ray the right croc and find a guy with a bullet inside him," Mursneh replied modestly, taking out his cigarettes.

"Won't happen," Hasbrok assured him. "We have people on the inside steering the investigation. Zailik can protest from his hospital bed all he wants, but it's still going to look like his men executed our 'ecological survey' team."

"And we shut up that turncoat Leibyla in the bargain," Mursneh said.

Hasbrok was readying one of his trademark cigarillos when he saw Mursneh frisking himself for a lighter. Hasbrok lit up, then handed Mursneh his pack of matches.

Mursneh nodded his thanks and lit his cigarette, then held the matches out to Hasbrok, who waved him off, saying, "Keep them."

As the two men smoked, Hasbrok told Mursneh he had another assignment for him. The plan was freshly conceived, concocted by Hasbrok in the aftermath of his conversation with Dujara. Once he'd relayed the information about the newly arrived American covert ops attempting to track down the missing JI double agents, Hasbrok explained, "I want you to skip the meeting and take a few of your best men back to the mainland and get to Wilki and Vohn before the Americans."

"And if we find them?"

"Take them alive if you can," Hasbrok said. "Same with the Americans, should you happen to cross paths with them."

"I'll get right on it." Mursneh finished his cigarette and stomped it out with the heel of his right boot.

"One more thing," Hasbrok told him. "I want this to be a plainclothes operation. Change out of your camos and don't take any weapons that can be traced back to GAM. I've talked with Dujara, and by the time you're in Banda Aceh, he'll have ID papers saying you're licensed with a private security company I've put on retainer for my own protection after the attack on Zailik."

Mursneh grinned. "Looks like I'm not the only one around here who knows how to cover his tracks."

"Great minds think alike, my friend," Hasbrok chuckled.

Mursneh excused himself to round up some of his men for the assignment on the mainland.

The team leader from Java had arrived and was with the others at the mess table. Hasbrok was on his way to join them when he heard a vehicle approaching on the narrow dirt road leading to the camp. The GAM strongman reflexively reached for the gun in his web holster, then relaxed when he recognized Carl Ryan's rental SUV.

"You're early," he told the former ambassador once Ryan got out of the vehicle. "I have business to attend to."

"I know," Ryan said, "but I have something I want you to add to the agenda."

Hasbrok smiled tightly, fighting back an urge to remind Ryan that it wasn't his place to tell him how to manage his affairs. Instead, he played along and asked, "What is it?"

Ryan eyed Hasbrok and told him, "I want you to arrange for me to be kidnapped and executed…."

10

Standing before the controls of the stolen cabin cruiser, Dihb Wilki yawned as he rolled his shoulders one way, then the other, trying to work loose the tightness he'd felt since casting the boat's owner over the side three miles off the Sumatran coast. That had been hours ago. He'd been at the helm ever since, guiding the boat on a steady southward course past the other islands and then finally changing course to navigate the waterway separating Sumatra from Java.

There were no provisions in the galley and Wilki was as hungry as he was exhausted, but his spirits rallied once he was through the strait and caught his first glimpse of the Java Sea, meaning he was nearly halfway to his destination. The boat's fuel tanks were nearly depleted, but Wilki felt he'd finally put enough distance between the stolen craft and the dock it had been taken from. Soon he would be able to take some time to relax.

When Vohn emerged from the sleeping quarters to check on things, he told her, "I know a safe place to stop and refuel just north of Jakarta. We can stretch our legs and get something to eat."

"Good," Vohn said. She'd been seasick most of the voyage and after her breakfast had come up on her, she'd spent the past few hours curled up in bed, riding out the nausea. The idea of food didn't appeal to her, but she suspected she'd feel better once she ate something.

"Are you any good at massages?" Wilki asked her. "My shoulders are in knots."

"I'm not your *geisha*," Vohn told him, an edge in her voice.

"Maybe not, but I'm your savior," Wilki reminded her. "You could show a little consideration."

Ti Vohn said nothing but moved forward, reaching for his shoulders. There was no passion to her touch as she kneaded the man's tense muscles, staring past Wilki at the Jakarta shoreline, which was lined with beach resorts and marinas filled with yachts and sailboats. She'd spent a couple of summers there during her college years, working as a hostess at a beachfront restaurant. How simple and uncomplicated her life had been then. What she wouldn't give to be able to go back in time and have those days to live over. She'd do a lot of things differently. No political science classes, no attending rallies or letting herself get caught up in the campus rhetoric. And, most of all, the moment Agmed Hasem laid eyes on her with that covetous look she'd mistaken for affection, she'd turn and walk the other way so that he would never come into her life.

"Hey, not so hard," Wilki complained.

She eased up on the man's shoulders, wondering how much longer she would be able to let Wilki think she believed everything he'd told her about taking them to hide out with some friends of his in Borneo. She knew better. While in the sleeping quarters earlier, she'd heard him arguing briefly with someone on his cell phone. She'd moved close to the door, hoping to hear the details of his conversation. Wilki had hung up moments after that, but not before she'd overheard him disclose his true intentions with her. "I'll bring her to Makassar and then you can do what you want with her," he'd told the other caller.

Hearing that, Vohn had figured out who he was talking to and trembled at the realization that her worst suspicions had been confirmed. Wilki may have had friends in Borneo, but she now knew that wasn't where he planned to take her. No, her would-be "savior" was instead taking her to her doom.

Wilki was taking her to Agmed Hasem....

Sulawesi, Indonesia

"THIS IS HOW I TREAT insubordination," Agmed Hasem told the somber-faced recruits he'd summoned to a barren patch of land behind one of the treatment plant's obsolete, camo-veiled holding tanks.

Guikin Daeng lay spread out on the ground before them, his corpse stiffened into an unnatural position by rigor mortis. He'd been stripped of his clothes and was barely recognizable thanks to the gun blast that had taken off the top of his head. Flies buzzed around the coagulated blood and gore and landed on his open, unseeing eyes. His flesh had taken on a chalky pallor and would soon begin to give off the stench of decomposition.

The recruits blanched at the gruesome sight, but Hasem wasn't finished with his demonstration. A few yards from Daeng's body, wearing waist-high wading boots and a protective face mask, one of the JI recruiter's senior aides stood behind a wheelbarrow piled high with a whitish, paste-like substance. At his feet was a two-gallon plastic jug filled with a urine-colored solution. On Hasem's signal, the aide steered the wheelbarrow forward, then raised the handles. The white sludge poured out onto the corpse and there was a faint sizzling sound as it quickly began to burn through Daeng's exposed flesh and feast on the tissue and organs beneath.

There were gasps and murmurs among the recruits as they watched with horrified wonder.

"Quicklime," Hasem explained, answering their unspoken question.

Once he'd emptied the wheelbarrow, the aide rolled it aside

and picked up the plastic jug. He unscrewed the cap and
began to circle the body, taking care to step clear of the quicklime trailing away. The jug contained hydrochloric acid, and
as the aide splashed it over Guikin Daeng, the body's disin-
tegration accelerated. Chemical wisps rose into the air and
began to drift toward the recruits, forcing them to step back.

Hasem ignored the men and stared intently at his computer
expert's dissolving corpse. The rage that led him to pull the
trigger on Daeng had yet to dissipate. If anything, it had increased, fuelled by his earlier phone conversation with Dihb
Wilki. The Banda Aceh informant had told him that he was
headed for Makassar and that he had Ti Vohn with him. He was
using the woman as a bargaining chip, offering her to Hasem
in exchange for a hundred thousand dollars and the promise
that he would not be killed by JI. Wilki had further said that he
was willing to go into hiding at the Makassar training camp,
where Hasem would be able to keep an eye on him. When
Hasem had again balked at the offer, there had been an
argument during which Hasem had made the mistake of men-
tioning Daeng's execution. Wilki had seized on the information, pointing out that his expertise with computers made him
an ideal candidate to replace the man Hasem had just killed.
When Hasem said he'd have to think the matter over, Wilki said
he was bringing Vohn to Makassar, regardless. It was as if the
informant knew that he'd made an offer Hasem couldn't
possibly turn down. And he was right, damn him.

The whole situation galled Hasem. Here he'd just slain one
of his most valuable men for daring to taunt him, and now he
was about to give credence to another underling incapable of
showing him proper deference. Ever since the call, he'd tried
to convince himself that accommodating Wilki would be
worth it for the chance to get his hands on Vohn. But the need
to have his power acknowledged had consumed him. He'd
hoped this demonstration for the recruits would satisfy that

need, and when he turned to them he saw that, indeed, to a man, each one of them seemed clearly convinced that Agmed Hasem was a force to be reckoned with.

But, in the time it took to look them over, Hasem quickly realized the extent to which he'd just blundered. He'd gotten his point across, but the men's respect had been induced, brought on by a fear that might well negate all the pandering he'd spent the past few weeks indulging them in. How could he expect them to blindly embrace the notion of suicidal martyrdom when he'd just shown them what a horrible thing it was to die?

An awkward silence had fallen over the proceedings. The recruits stared at Hasem, unsure of what he would do or say next. His own aide, peering through his thick protective goggles, was looking at him questioningly.

"Dismissed!" Hasem blurted, his voice cracking.

The recruits were only too glad for the demonstration to be over, and it was all they could do not to break out running as they headed back to their barracks inside the water plant. Hasem glared at them, then turned on his aide.

"What are you looking at?!" he demanded.

The other man quickly glanced away from Hasem, turning his attention back to Daeng's corpse, which had been reduced to a mass of stray bones and smoldering tissue. Hasem followed the man's gaze, and as he stared at what had become of Guikin Daeng, he suddenly found himself beset by an unwanted reminder of his own mortality.

Banda Aceh

"NOTHING LIKE A WALK on the wild side, eh, mate?" Shelby Ferstera said, his voice dripping with sarcasm. "Plenty of one-stop shopping here if you're looking to buy your way into trouble."

He and Mack Bolan were on foot, dressed to look like wayward tourists prowling for vice, their pistols concealed in web holsters tucked beneath loose shirts. They were a few blocks from downtown, making their way along one of many unkempt back alleys that served as stomping grounds for Banda Aceh's underworld. Condoms, spent syringes, tinfoil hash pipes and other drug paraphernalia were visible amid the trash littering the asphalt, and nearly every side alley they'd passed had been populated by some combination of prostitutes, drug peddlers and derelicts with notions of robbery in their hungry eyes.

"Guys like Wilki probably feel right at home here," Bolan said, sizing up each questionable character they came across, matching faces with those on the mug shots he and Ferstera had reviewed at the offices of Police Chief Irwandi Alkihn. John Kissinger and Jack Grimaldi were engaged in a similar search a few blocks away. The Executioner had been in constant contact with them using an ear-bud transponder that easily passed as a high-end cell phone accessory. Like Bolan and Ferstera, over the past couple of hours the two men had managed to track down several of Dihb Wilki's underground contacts, but so far no one had given up any knowledge of the street hustler's whereabouts since the attack on Zailik. They were running out of leads.

"I hate to be a spoilsport, but if this next place doesn't pan out, I'm going to turn things over to you," Ferstera said as they cleared the alley and waited out traffic on a busy cross street. "I have funeral arrangements to tend to."

Bolan nodded. This was the first time all day that Ferstera had made mention of the men he'd lost in the assassination attempt, but the Executioner knew the toll had to be weighing on him.

When he saw a worrisome, faraway look come into Ferstera's eyes, Bolan decided to change the subject.

"I hear one of the officers from the motorcade wants to join up with you," Bolan said.

"That's right," Ferstera said, welcoming the distraction. "Muhtar Yeilam. His brother was the one who got blown to bits trying to get that bomber away from the governor's car. He wants payback."

"Understandable," Bolan said.

"Thing is, he got himself pretty banged up, too," Ferstera said. "We'll run a background check then see what we can do once he's back on his feet. At this point, we sure as hell can use all the good men we can get."

Across the street was a run-down strip mall where one of Dihb Wilki's contacts fenced stolen goods through a pawn shop. Bolan and Ferstera were headed for the shop when Bolan's ear-bud bleated.

"We're at the old amusement park," Kissinger reported. "We've found some friends of Wilki's. We'll check things out, then meet up with you at—"

Kissinger's voice was cut off by the staccato barking of an assault rifle.

Bolan tapped his ear-bud. "You still there?"

There was no answer. Bolan turned to Ferstera, who was already reaching under his shirt for his Browning 9 mm.

"I heard it," the Australian said, gesturing with his head at the upper arch of a Ferris wheel visible two blocks away. "Sounds like we've got a live one...."

Once Hoa Mursneh and his five fellow GAM militiamen had reached the mainland, they found two nondescript Hyundai sedans waiting for them, courtesy of Intelligence Director Dujara. Falsified papers identifying the men as operatives for Indo-Tech Private Security Services were stashed in the glove compartments, and both cars were equipped with dashboard transceivers to allow them to stay in contact with Dujara. Mursneh took two men with him and dispatched the other three in the second car. The two groups split Wilki's list of contacts between them.

Mursneh was en route to check out the first name on the contact list Dujara had provided when he and the other car were forced to pull off to the side of the road near Museum Negeri. A trio of police cars raced past, sirens howling. Moments later, Dujara was on the transceiver.

"Something's going down at one of the contact sites—the old amusement park," the intelligence director reported. "I'm on my way to check things out."

"We'll meet you there," Mursneh responded.

It took Mursneh ten minutes to reach the amusement park. By then the gun fight was over. Dujara had already arrived and told Mursneh and his men to keep their distance while he entered the park to find out what had happened.

As he waited Mursneh let his mind wander as he stared out the window at a pair of ambulances being waved in to the amusement park by police officers guarding the entrance. Mursneh had mixed emotions about his assignment. Granted, there was less danger involved in what amounted to detective work, but it wasn't his strong suit. He was trained for combat and his instincts were honed for battlefield decisions. With any luck, whatever had transpired at the amusement park would lead to Wilki and Vohn being tracked down without the need to pound a lot of pavement and negotiate with Wilki's contacts for information.

Mursneh was the first to admit he had no finesse when it came to conversation. When dealing with someone wary of passing along information, his preference was to throttle the contact until they agreed to cooperate or just shoot them and move on to the next name on the list. Neither option would likely sit well with Hasbrok, however, causing Mursneh to fall into disfavor and lose the ground he'd just gained by carrying off the executions in Gunung Leuser. All in all, he had the uneasy feeling that he was jeopardizing his chances of rising a few tiers in the pecking order should Hasbrok be elected governor. Of course, had he refused the assignment, his loyalty would have come into question, leaving him in even worse straits.

Damned if you do, damned if you don't, Mursneh thought to himself.

Mursneh glanced to his right and saw Shelby Ferstera leaving through the side entrance to the park. With him were three other white men. They seemed to be in a hurry, taking long, quick strides as they crossed the street and headed away from Mursneh. Once they passed by a two-story manufacturing plant, he lost sight of them. The other men in the car with him were on the alert as well.

"Those must be the Americans. Shouldn't we follow them?" one of them asked.

It seemed like the right course, but Mursneh hesitated, waiting to hear from Dujara. His patience waned quickly, however, and less than a minute later he was on the road, anxious to pick up the trail before it went cold. He called the other car and put them on the move as well.

Two blocks later, Mursneh spotted the men piling into an SUV. The vehicle was pulling out into traffic when Dujara's call finally came through.

"Sorry for the delay," Dujara reported, "but I had to twist a few arms to get some info—"

"Never mind that," Mursneh interrupted. "The Americans look like they're on to something and are about to head out of here. Am I supposed to follow them or what?"

"Go ahead, but stay back and don't worry if you lose them," Dujara told the commando. "They got one of Wilki's contacts to talk. I know where they're headed…."

Stony Man Farm

"THEY'RE HEADED FOR a hunting lodge a few miles west of the city," Huntington Wethers reported. "Apparently it's owned by the uncle of one of the gang members who had dealings with this Dihb Wilki fellow."

Wethers was the third member of Aaron Kurtzman's cybernetic crew at Stony Man Farm. A tall African-American with graying hair around the temples, Wethers looked every bit the college professor he'd once been. He'd just reported for work and taken over Carmen Delahunt's workload while she went for some much-needed sleep. The Executioner had just reported in following a skirmish with some low-level criminals at an amusement park in Banda Aceh.

"Let's hope something comes of it," Barbara Price said as she paced between Wethers's workstation and those being used by Kurtzman and Tokaido. "If Wilki and Ti Vohn are as hard to find as Carl Ryan, this whole thing could turn into a wild-goose chase."

They still had a shortage of leads in the search for Ryan, and also lacked any clear link between him and either the attack on Governor Zailik or the ambush murders at the nature preserve in Gunung Leuser. She and the others were convinced there had to be a connection, but without more to go on, she had to fight off a gnawing sense that answers would continue to elude them.

"Still nothing on the counterfeit ID front?" she asked Kurtzman.

He shook his head. He stretched and yawned, then refilled his coffee cup. "We knew that would be a long shot."

"Long shots are all we have right now," Price said.

Once they'd wrapped up the call with Bolan, Wethers had picked up where he'd left off, skimming through the hundreds of computer files Carmen Delahunt had culled by running Carl Ryan's name through myriad databases. The task was mundane, but while performing it, something occurred to him.

"Did Ryan have computer access while he was in prison?" Wethers asked, directing the question to no one in particular.

"Wouldn't surprise me," Kurtzman replied. "They put him up at one of those Club Fed joints that go heavy on privileges."

"The FBI's sent some people there to talk with the other inmates," Price said. "I can have them look into it. My understanding, though, is that if prisoners have computer access, they're given a special log-in and all their entries are screened for content. Anything suspicious gets flagged and reviewed."

"That would make sense," Wethers said, "but if he was able to go online, there might be something the folks there overlooked."

"It's worth a try," Price said, heading for the nearest phone. "If it turns out he used a computer, we should be able to get a download on his—"

"Bingo!" Akira Tokaido interrupted, leaning back in his chair and pumping a fist in the air. "I've got some serious brownie points coming."

"Identi-Kit match?" Price asked, heading toward Tokaido's station.

Tokaido drew Price's attention to his computer screen. On the monitor was the simulated image depicting Carl Ryan as bald and clean-shaven.

"Private airfield about three miles from the apartment Ryan rented when he got out," Tokaido said, passing along the report he'd just read. "A state trooper showed the printout to the hangar crew and came up empty, but he stopped for coffee at a diner across the street and hit paydirt with one of the waitresses."

"We're supposed to care that some trooper got his horns clipped?" Kurtzman said, wheeling over to join Price and Tokaido.

"As if," Tokaido said with a smirk. Pointing at Ryan's simulated likeness, he went on. "She waited on him and a pilot about a week ago. The way they shut up whenever she passed by their table got her radar up, so she made note of the few things she managed to overhear. Wasn't much, but there was something about 'Malaysia' and a 'switching to a puddle jumper.'"

"That could be plenty," Price said.

"Let me finish, okay?" Tokaido said. "She gave a good enough description of the pilot to get him tracked down and hauled in for interrogation. He cracked easy and copped to flying Ryan to Malaysia while he was on a cargo run in a DC-3. Ryan wanted to go on to Sumatra but the guy was on a tight schedule so he arranged to have Ryan hook up with a pilot buddy of his who had a small Cessna."

"A puddle jumper," Kurtzman said.

Tokaido nodded.

"Ryan wasn't using his real name, was he?" Price asked.

Tokaido shook his head. "Didn't use a name at all," he said. "He coughed up enough dead presidents to fly on the sly and keep the pilot from asking any questions."

"Like where he was headed and why," Price said.

"Yeah, well, that's the bad news," Tokaido said. "So far, we got *nada* beyond Ryan switching planes in Malaysia and wanting to bop over to Sumatra."

"Maybe so," Kurtzman said, "but we've narrowed the search. I take it somebody's already checking out the airfield in Malaysia."

Tokaido brought up a document and looked it over. "Yeah. CIA's covering our end of it. They're looking for that second pilot, too."

"What do you know? Progress," Price said.

"Speaking of progress, I may have something as well," Wethers called out from his station. He'd been listening to Tokaido's report and, on a hunch, had added Sumatra to the data file Delahunt had compiled. A listing of fifty-seven entries had been quickly narrowed down to five, all of them related to an interview Ryan had granted the *International Herald*, two years before his arrest.

"Let's have it," Kurtzman called out.

"One moment," Wethers said, holding up a hand. He skimmed through the longest of the articles using the same search words, quickly gleaning the information he was looking for.

"It turns out one of Ryan's favorite hobbies is scuba diving," Weathers reported. "It mentions a few of his favorite places to go and most of them are in Java, near the American embassy. But he also said that when he really wanted to get away he'd fly to a place called Gapang. It's on Weh Island, just north of Banda Aceh."

"And just a puddle jump away from Malaysia," Price added.

Gapang, Weh Island, Indonesia

CARL RYAN SAT ALONE on the balcony of his rental condo, nursing a drink as he stared out at Gapang Bay. The water glit-

tered in the sunlight and a handful of sailboats were out taking
advantage of a stiff afternoon breeze. Off to his left, near a
cove dotted with raised coral formations, a small hydroplane
had just drifted down and landed on the choppy surf. Ryan
was reminded of the similar aircraft that had brought him to
the island in the dead of night less than a week earlier. That
plane was now resting at the bottom of the bay, more than a
mile out from the dropoff where Ryan's sealed container still
lay wedged in its hiding place. Ryan had put a bullet through
the pilot's head moments before he'd parachuted from the
cockpit and the plane had crashed into the sea well before the
former ambassador had touched down in the water, wearing
a life preserver that kept him afloat until Anhi Hasbrok retrieved him in his cabin cruiser. That had been the last time
things had gone according to the master plan Ryan had pieced
together during his long months in prison. Ever since then,
extenuating circumstances had forced him to change his
strategy, modifying certain aspects and throwing out others
entirely. The extent to which he found himself improvising
troubled him, as it widened the margin for error and increased
the odds that he might be unable to see his vendetta through.

Ryan was lost in his dark thoughts when the door to the
balcony slid open. Hasbrok stepped out, carrying a bottle of
Chivas Regal and a glass filled with ice.

"Brooding again, my friend?" Hasbrok chuckled. He held
the bottle out. Ryan waved it away. Hasbrok shrugged and
poured himself a drink, then took a seat next to the fugitive,
propping his feet on the balcony railing.

"I thought you might like to know we're hot on the trail of
the JI agents," Hasbrok told Ryan. He quickly spelled out
what he'd learned from Dujara about the altercation at the
amusement park and the disclosure of the hunting lodge Dihb
Wilki and Vohn had fled to after the assassination attempt on
Governor Zailik.

"My teams know the back roads better than the Americans," he concluded. "They should have no problem getting to the cabin first."

"And did Dujara manage to find out who these Americans are yet?" Ryan wanted to know. "Or why they were sent here?"

Hasbrok smiled at his colleague. "So we're back to that."

"I take it the answer is no," Ryan replied.

"Does it really matter all that much which agency they work for?" Hasbrok asked. "CIA, Delta Force, Special Forces…it's all the same. And if you were their main target and they knew where you were, do you really think they'd bother chasing after some low-level functionaries for Jemaah Islamiyah?"

"Maybe they've just allowed themselves to get sidetracked," Ryan countered. "Given all the men Densus 88 lost in that attack, maybe they figure it's politically correct to chip in and help with the payback."

"If you say so."

Ryan finished his drink and changed the subject.

"What about that other assignment?" he asked.

"Nothing yet," Hasbrok said. "And I wouldn't count much on that one coming through. I mean, really, what are the chances of my men coming across a transient American who could pass as your double?"

"I told you where to have them look," Ryan said. "When I was ambassador, I had thorough lists of where our indigents usually wound up and—"

"Yes, yes, I know," Hasbrok interrupted. "Those are the places I sent my men. But, be realistic."

"It doesn't have to be a twin," Ryan said. "The same body type and a passing resemblance will be enough."

"My men are doing what they can," Hasbrok assured his colleague. "And if they find someone, they'll see to it that we get our hands on him so we can carry out this crazy scheme of yours."

Ryan was about to vent his frustrations further but held himself in check. It didn't matter, ultimately, if Hasbrok thought the plan of faking his execution was far-fetched or not. All that mattered was that it be carried out in a way that would convince the United States he was out of the picture once and for all. Once he was certain that he was no longer the object of a focused manhunt, he would finally be able to get things back on track.

Hasbrok sipped his drink, then casually asked Ryan, "Have you thought about how you're going to pay me for all this work I'm doing for you?"

Ryan's temper flared anew.

"Let's be clear," he told Hasbrok. "You're doing 'all this work' to repay *me*. I thought you understood that."

Hasbrok nodded. "I understand that I'm indebted to you, yes. I haven't forgotten the way you helped make us politically viable."

"And, in exchange, you promised the use of your men if I needed them."

"That's true, but it wasn't a blank check," Hasbrok said. "So far I've fished you out of the water when you first came back here, then I saw to it that we got rid of some people who could link us. And now I've got men looking to find someone you can kill to throw your own trained hounds off your scent. All this, and there's still the whole matter of you wanting to carry out your revenge against the new ambassador. Do you have any idea what that's going to entail?"

"I know exactly what it entails," Ryan said. "And as long as we're counting favors, let me remind you that if I hadn't greased the skids for GAM to gain political recognition, by now you'd have been hunted down by Densus 88 or the Indonesian military and either thrown in a cell or trotted out before a firing squad."

Hasbrok was silent. He knew Ryan had a point, and there

was little to be gained by arguing with the man. After all, once he learned where the ambassador was hiding his take from the tsunami fund, the matter of being paid would be immaterial. Hasbrok would get rid of Ryan, help himself to as much of the stolen fortune as he wanted, then throw a few crumbs to Dujara. But Ryan clearly wasn't about to drink enough to loosen his tongue as to the whereabouts of his pilfered millions. Hasbrok would have to find another way to go about it.

The GAM strongman had turned off the ringer on his cell phone, but when he felt its insistent vibration inside his shirt pocket, he took the call, welcoming the interruption.

After exchanging a few words with the other caller, Hasbrok folded the phone and slipped it back in his pocket.

"I owe you an apology, it seems," he told Ryan. "My men have found your double after all."

12

Banda Aceh

The hunting cabin was a shabby, two-room affair with no electricity and few amenities. The main room had a small wood-burning stove, a card table with uneven legs, two folding chairs and a coffee table upon which rested an outdated phone book with half its pages missing. The other, smaller room was empty save for a rumpled bed, scattered rat droppings and a rumpled towel lying on the floor near the adjacent bathroom. As such, it didn't take Hoa Mursneh and his men long to search the place and realize the trip had been in vain.

"They're long gone," Mursneh said flatly, holstering his pistol.

"If they were ever here at all," one of the other men added, dragging a fingertip through the dust layering the card table. Another man was roaming through the other room; the rest were outside searching the grounds around the cabin.

"There were fresh prints out front," Mursneh reminded the other man. "Tread marks, too. And the towel in the bedroom is still damp. They were here."

The team leader was mulling over his next move when he heard a commotion outside. He went to the window and stared out. One of his men had just emerged from the nearby forest and was pointing behind him as he spoke to the other commandos.

When he went outside, Mursneh learned that a car had been found parked in the woods twenty yards from the cabin.

"Keys were in the ignition, but it wouldn't start," explained the man who'd discovered the vehicle. Mursneh asked for the car's make. It was a burgundy late-model Honda Accord.

"Wilki's," Mursneh said, recalling the information packet Dujara had left for him. He tried to figure out what the discovery meant. Ti Vohn's car was still at her apartment, which meant she and Wilki had come here in the Accord. Had they set out on foot? Met someone else? Or were they still nearby, hiding somewhere out in the woods?

"Anything in the car?" Mursneh asked.

"Nothing out of the ordinary."

Mursneh deliberated going to check for himself but decided against it.

"Let's get out of here before the Americans show up," he told the others, heading for the car he'd driven to the cabin.

Once the men had piled into their cars, Mursneh let the other car lead the way back down the single-lane dirt path that had brought them to the cabin. Once they reached the main road, he'd put a call through to Hasbrok and tell him they'd hit a dead end. With any luck, Hasbrok would call off the search and just tell Mursneh to return to the island. The last thing he wanted was to be sent back to Banda Aceh to sniff around for more leads.

The GAM crews were halfway to the main road when they rounded a curve and saw that the way before them was blocked by an approaching vehicle. Staring past the lead car, Mursneh recognized the SUV that Shelby Ferstera and his American sidekicks had gotten into after leaving the amusement park.

"Damn it," Mursneh groaned, reaching for his gun. He suddenly had a situation on his hands.

"SOMETHING TELLS ME this isn't Wilki's entourage," Jack Grimaldi said, slowing the SUV to a stop ten yards from the front bumper of the lead Hyundai. He kept the car in Drive, ready to move again if need be.

The Executioner was riding up front next to Grimaldi. He couldn't see the occupants of the second vehicle, but there was no sign of Wilki or Vohn in the car directly before him.

"Might be JI," he guessed, reaching for his Beretta. Raising his voice so John Kissinger and Shelby Ferstera could hear him in the backseat, he added, "Whoever they are, they're armed."

There was a tense lull as none of the cars moved. Then the lead Hyundai suddenly lurched forward, veering toward a narrow ribbon of wild grass separating the road from the surrounding forest. They were clearly hoping to squeeze past the SUV.

"I don't think so," Grimaldi said, jerking hard on the steering wheel as he goosed the accelerator. He cut the Hyundai off and clipped it with enough force to spin it sideways across the road, effectively blocking the car behind it.

Bolan was already getting out of the SUV when the vehicles collided. The impact threw him to the ground, but he landed on his feet and quickly regained his balance. When the driver of the crumpled Hyundai threw his door open and scrambled out, pistol clenched in his right fist, Bolan didn't wait for the man to get a bead on him. He fired a three-round burst. One slug glanced off the Hyundai's door frame but the others found flesh, burrowing into the driver's chest. The man spun away from the sedan and fell dead in the tall grass.

Inside the SUV, Grimaldi ducked low as another of Mursneh's men, still inside the Hyundai, fired through his side window, blowing out the SUV's windshield. Behind Grimaldi, Kissinger and Ferstera bounded out either side of the vehicle, ready to join the firefight.

Grimaldi backed up, then shifted into drive, ready to ram the Hyundai a second time so that the enemy wouldn't be able to take cover behind it. Easing down on the accelerator, he muttered, "I hope the insurance is paid up on this sucker...."

YEARS EARLIER, before he'd taken up a full-time life of crime, Hoa Mursneh had been a parking attendant at a posh nightclub. He'd learned, for sport, how to back up cars at ridiculous speeds and squeeze them into tight spaces without a nick. It was a skill that had stayed with him.

"Hang on," he shouted to the other men in the car with him. After slamming the Hyundai into Reverse, he gave it enough gas to spit dirt out from under the tires as he sped backward, away from the fracas. A gunshot intended for him punctured the front windshield and bored into his headrest as he cranked the steering wheel, slammed on the brakes, then cranked the wheel the other way and landed back on the dirt path leading to the abandoned cabin. Behind him, he saw that the other car had been shoved sideways along the road, scattering men behind it. One of his men went down, and Mursneh feared the others would soon follow. He was intent on keeping himself off the casualty list.

Now that his car was moving in a straight line, the GAM lackey in the seat behind Mursneh turned and fired a shot through the rear windshield, clearing the glass so that he could direct his next volley at the enemy. He fired an autoburst at Shelby Ferstera, who had just downed one of the men in the other Hyundai. The Australian reeled, dropping his gun, one hand grabbing at his shoulder. The gunman was about to finish Ferstera off when return fire from another party nailed him in the neck, taking him out of the fight.

Another round, meanwhile, took a large enough bite from one of the rear tires to send the Hyundai into a skid. Cursing, Mursneh grappled with the steering wheel, countering the skid enough to keep the car on the path. He knew the car wouldn't be able to take him much farther, though. After scanning the forest on either side of him, he veered off the path and drove between a pair of gnarled, foot-thick trees dripping with inch-thick vines. It was a tight squeeze and the man riding beside him shrieked when the side view mirror was torn free and the tree's bark clawed at the Hyundai's paint job with a sound like the world's largest fingernails scraping across a blackboard.

The forest floor was soft and uneven, slowing the Hyundai as Mursneh tried to drive his way through the woods. Drooping vines slapped at the roof and windshield as Mursneh tried to keep going. Thirty yards farther, the ground abruptly pitched down to the bank of a slow-moving stream. The Hyundai hurtled down the slope and came to an abrupt halt when its front end burrowed into the loamy embankment.

Mursneh's ribs ached where they'd pounded against the steering wheel, but he was otherwise unharmed, as was the man beside him.

"Out!" he ordered, yanking out his pistol.

He lurched from the car, mud pulling at his shoes the moment he set foot on the embankment. He wrenched his knee, pulling himself free, then slogged his way into the knee-deep stream, seeking out a cluster of boulders on the other side. The other man was right behind him, but a few yards shy of the rocks he was struck by a round fired from the top of the slope. The man let out a sudden gasp and fell face-first into the water, turning it crimson.

Mursneh took cover behind the rocks, fuming. This was one hell of a sorry place to make a last stand. But there was nothing he could do about it but wait to see how many of the enemy he could take out before they got to him.

LEAVING THE OTHERS to contend with the enemy on the road, Mack Bolan charged into the forest, veering around trees and bulky ferns as he carved a course toward the second car. He'd spotted it just as it plunged over the bank. When its surviving occupants bounded out and tried to flee through the water, he took one of them down.

As the remaining foe scrambled behind some boulders, Bolan broke from cover and continued forward, brushing aside the tall ferns in his path. When the man rose from behind the rocks and fired Bolan's way, the Executioner dropped from view amid the fauna. Bullets sawed through the ferns around him as he began to crawl across the soft earth. He knew he was giving up precious seconds, and once he was within range of the nearest tree, he took his chances and got to his feet. The man fired again, rattling the tree's bark, then turned heel and bolted up the far side of the creek bed into a thick copse of trees. Bolan returned fire, barely missing his target before the man disappeared from view.

Breaking from cover, the Executioner broke into a full run, glancing around him for some way to close the gap. Holstering his Beretta, he increased his stride as he drew near the incline leading down to the stream bed. Just before reaching the slope, Bolan grabbed hold of what looked to be the sturdiest of the vines dangling from the nearest tree. He pushed off at an angle and was suddenly airborne. The vine held up under his weight, allowing him to swing outward over the crashed Hyundai and fallen shooter.

Once he'd cleared the stream, Bolan let go and dropped to the far embankment. The soft loam cushioned his landing as he collapsed his legs, then quickly straightened them. With the Beretta nestled back in his curled fist, the Executioner resumed his pursuit, advancing into the dense forest.

I'VE GOT TARZAN after me, Mursneh thought as he glanced back and saw the big American swing across the creek.

Mursneh thought he had an edge on his pursuer and didn't want to squander it trying to fire through the trees. Rather than betray his position, he continued to flee, zig-zagging through the obstacles. The overhead canopy blocked the sun, making it hard for him to get his bearings, and though he thought he was headed for the main road, fifty yards later, when he came upon a clearing, he realized he'd backtracked to the cabin. He could hear his pursuer in the distance, slowly closing in. Gambling, Mursneh broke into the clearing, leaving himself an easy target as he raced back to the cabin. The place was anything but a fortress, but if he could get through the door, he figured he could use the structure for cover and wait by the window for his adversary to show himself.

He'd made it as far as the door when a shot rang out and a 9 mm round lodged itself just below his right shoulder blade. Howling, he careened off the door frame and staggered inside, his entire right side throbbing. He blocked out the pain and kicked the door shut, then went to the front window, shattering the glass with the butt of his pistol. All he needed was for his pursuer to follow him out of the forest so he could have a clear shot at him.

"Come on," he whispered through clenched teeth. "You want me, come and get me."

Mursneh surveyed the clearing.

Seconds passed. Mursneh felt himself weakening and he could feel the blood trailing down his side. He knew he needed to dispense with the enemy quickly so that he could try to stop the bleeding. His foe wasn't playing along, however. The clearing remained vacant and there was no sign of movement at the edge of the forest. The bastard was waiting him out.

Mursneh had to fight off a feeling of light-headedness. The gun began to feel heavier in his hand and his forehead was covered with cold sweat. Mursneh drew in a deep breath, then another. The sweat rolled past his brow and stung his eyes. He forced himself to keep them open, focused on the clearing.

Mursneh was clasping his left hand over the right to help

keep the gun steady when he was startled by the sound of glass shattering in the other room. He whirled, taking aim through the doorway separating the two rooms. There was no follow-up sound, no sign that his pursuer was attempting to crawl in through the window.

He's baiting me, Mursneh thought. Trying to throw me off guard.

The gunman fought back his urge to investigate and stayed near the window. His nerves were on edge, though, and when seconds later he heard a series of thuds overhead, followed by a dribbling sound on both sides of the roof's crest, Mursneh instinctively pivoted and took aim at the ceiling.

Even as it flashed through the gunman's mind that he was being duped, the front door suddenly swung inward, kicked open by Mursneh's pursuer, who charged into the cabin, ready to take advantage of the diversion he'd created.

Mursneh turned to the big man and their eyes locked as the Indonesian swung his gun around and tried to get off a shot. He was too late. The Executioner had the drop on him, and before he could squeeze the trigger, a bullet slammed into Mursneh's chest, obliterating his sternum and laying waste to his heart. His gun clattered to the floor, unfired, as he sagged to one side, crashing off the coffee table and onto the hardwood floor.

"THEIR ID PAPERS SAY they're private security agents," John Kissinger reported once he and the others had caught up with Bolan. "And one of them had same list of contacts we were checking out."

They were standing in front of the cabin. The battered SUV, still roadworthy despite the damage to its front end, was parked nearby. One of the rear passenger doors was open and Shelby Ferstera sat on the floor of the vehicle, feet out and resting on the ground, a makeshift compress pressed against his shoulder wound to staunch the bleeding. Jack Grimaldi had already checked the perimeter and found Dihb Wilki's abandoned Honda. He was now inside the cabin, working around Hoa Mursneh's corpse as he looked for clues as to the whereabouts of Wilki and Vohn. Bolan had gone through Mursneh's pockets, coming up with a cell phone as well as the GAM henchman's cigarettes and a pack of matches from the Bay Retreat Hotel.

"The cell phone's disposable," Bolan said. "No entries, nothing to trace."

"Same with the couple we found," Kissinger said. "Both cars had dash transceivers, but playing bumper car knocked one of 'em out of commission. We waited a couple of minutes to see if anyone would try to touch base on the other one, but no dice."

"We can try again later." Bolan held out the book of matches. "Only a couple missing, so odds are he just picked it up."

"Weh Island," Kissinger murmured, looking at the hotel address listed on the matchbook. "That's just across the water from here, right?"

Bolan nodded. "Probably his last stop before they came here."

"Should be easy enough to check out," Kissinger said.

"Same with this security outfit they supposedly belonged to," Bolan said. "I'm guessing it's a front."

"My guess, too," Kissinger agreed.

"And as far as that contact list goes," Bolan said, "it had to have come from somebody inside the loop with the police here."

"The chief?" Kissinger asked.

"Hard to say," Bolan replied.

"How about we hook that transceiver up to the SUV and see if we get any bites?" Kissinger suggested.

"Worth a shot," Bolan said. "In the meantime, let's run with what we have and see where it leads."

"I'll fire up the computer," Kissinger said, gesturing at the SUV, where the men's laptop was stashed in the back with their spare ammo. "The Bear should be able to cough up something."

Grimaldi had emerged from the cabin in time to overhear the exchange. "Before you do that," he interjected, "there's something else worth throwing in the hopper."

The Stony Man flyboy was holding the ravaged phone book he'd come across in the main room of the cabin. As he flipped through it, he explained, "There's a ton of pages missing, most of them from the end of the book. Most likely they wound up in the fireplace as kindling."

"But there are some missing pages elsewhere?" Bolan asked.

Grimaldi nodded, flipping to the sections in question. "One's from a section with pictures of cars. I'm thinking taxis."

"Makes sense," Kissinger said.

Grimaldi continued, "The other page looks like it's from the listings for Internet services."

"Or maybe Internet cafés," Bolan added.

"Could be," Grimaldi said.

"Okay," Bolan said. "Wilki's car breaks down once he makes it here with Vohn. They probably both have cell phones, so they take the 'taxi' page from the phone book and start calling as they hike back to the main road."

"And one of their first stops is going to be an Internet café," Grimaldi concluded. Bolan nodded.

"The question is why?" Kissinger said.

"Get Bear on it. Taxi logs and the addresses of the nearest Internet cafés. Hopefully they'll come up with something by the time we get Ferstera to the hospital."

"What about these guys?" Kissinger asked, waving the ID papers taken off the slain goon squad. "If we call the cops, we might wind up tipping off whoever's in on it with them."

"They probably gave word they were headed here," Bolan said. "When they don't report in, somebody'll come looking for them. Let's leave it at that. It'll give us time to see if these leads pan out."

13

Jakarta

Plans for a new port facility mere minutes from the nation's capital had turned the once-slumbering coastal hamlet of Marunda into a boomtown. Dihb Wilki's associate Sabam Sonhs had gotten in on the ground floor, pouring drug profits into an equipment-rental facility located on the waterfront less than a mile from where construction crews were working overtime to crowd the harbor with piers and warehouses. The establishment was originally intended to serve as a front for money-laundering as well as a way station for drug shipments bound for Jakarta, but the legitimate business had taken off to such an extent that Sonhs barely had time for illicit pursuits. He knew it was best, however, to remain on good terms with his criminal acquaintances, so when Wilki had called ahead saying he needed to make a quick no-questions-asked refueling stop, Sonhs had warily obliged, inviting his longtime colleague to make use of the pumps at his small, private dock.

Wilki had shown up with the stolen cabin cruiser a little over an hour earlier. While Sonhs had his crew attended to the boat, filling its tanks and running a maintenance check to ensure that it was seaworthy enough to make it to Agmed Hasem's training camp in Makassar, Wilki had taken Vohn up the road to a newly built convenience mall. The woman's nausea had abated now that they were on solid land and she surprised herself at how easily she was able to devour orders of calamari and rice as well as most of a seaweed-and-scampi casserole.

Beyond the fact that she was famished, Ti Vohn had kept her mouth full as an excuse to avoid an extended conversation with Wilki. She figured the less said between them, the less likely she might somehow tip him off that she'd overheard his conversation with Hasem. She also wanted time to think through her situation. A part of her wanted to find a way to give Wilki the slip and make a run for it. On the way to the mall she'd taken note of all the hectic activity throughout Marunda. If she could somehow get away from Wilki, she thought she might be able to lose him in the crowded streets. But what then? It seemed that Wilki's friend was well-connected around town. Would she really be able to avoid being tracked down? And if she did run, Wilki would likely realize she knew he was intent on selling her out to Hasem, making him all the more determined to find her. No, there had to be another way.

Wilki, as it turned out, wasn't in a talkative mood. Once he'd wolfed down his beef satay, he was content to sit back in his chair and smoke cigarettes over coffee as he watched a soccer game on a large television mounted on the wall across from them. It galled her that he could be so nonchalant.

Once the game ended, Wilki stubbed out his cigarette and took out some of the money he'd taken after killing the boat's owner.

"Let's go," he told Vohn, tossing a few bills on the tabletop. "The boat's probably ready."

Leaving the eatery, Vohn noticed the pharmacy next door and told Wilki she wanted to get something to keep her from getting seasick once again.

"Good idea," Wilki said. "I could use a couple of things, too."

Inside the pharmacy, Wilki split off from her to find his provisions. The medicine aisle was close to the door and Vohn was tempted again to make a run for it. She fought back the urge in favor of the plan she'd just concocted.

Once she'd found the antinausea medication, she looked over the sleeping pills.

She went to the checkout counter without waiting for Wilki, but he caught up with her as the clerk was ringing up her purchases.

"Sleeping pills?" he asked.

"The less I'm awake out there, the better," she reasoned.

"Maybe so," Wilki said, setting down a jar of instant coffee and a half-dozen energy drinks. "With me, it's the other way around."

Wilki paid for both their purchases. As he was waiting for change, a burly delivery man ambled up, adding a stack of evening papers to the stand next to the counter. The front page heralded the latest developments in the failed assassination attempt on Governor Zailik. The main photo under the headlines showed Zailik being wheeled out of the hospital, and the caption featured an excerpt from the governor's statement denouncing Jemaah Islamiyah.

There were two other photos in the far right column, cropped off by the centerfold. When Wilki flipped the paper over, he saw that the photos below the crease were of him and Vohn, positioned next to a story explaining that they were "suspects at large."

Ti Vohn was looking at the photos as well. She glanced up as Wilki was stuffing his change in his pockets, gesturing with his head toward the door. She started out, poking her hair back up under the hat she'd first donned for disguise back in Banda Aceh.

Once they were back on the sidewalk, Wilki said, "We're cutting it close now."

There was a sidewalk vendor down the block. Wilki bought himself a baseball cap and pulled it down tight over his head so the bill would help obscure his features. Walking as fast as they could without drawing attention to themselves, they hurried back to the equipment rental facility.

The boat was waiting for them at the dock.

So was Sabam Sonhs. He was holding a copy of the same newspaper Wilki and Vohn had just seen.

"No wonder you were so anxious for my help," Sonhs told Wilki with a knowing smile.

"Is the boat ready?" Wilki asked.

Sonhs nodded. "I forgot to mention the high cost of fuel these days."

Wilki was in no mood to haggle. Without hesitation, he pulled out his stolen bankroll and handed it over, telling Sonhs, "There should be enough there to keep your mouth shut."

Sonhs fingered the bills. Satisfied, he stepped to one side and gestured to the boat. "You were never here," he said.

Wilki helped Vohn aboard, then handed her the bag with his coffee and energy drinks so that he could untether the boat from its moorings. "Put the drinks in the fridge," he told her.

Ti Vohn did as she was told, then caught up with Wilki at the helm. She would retreat to the bunk quarters and pretend to sleep later. For now, she wanted to pay close attention as Wilki worked the controls, guiding the boat from the dock and back out into the Java Sea. There would be a time, soon enough, when it would be up to her to commandeer the boat on her own.

U.S. Embassy, Jakarta

"That's good to know," Ambassador Robert Gardner said. He was an urbane-looking forty-eight-year-old California native wearing one of a dozen tailor-made suits he'd had fitted with shoulder pads to offset his prematurely stoop-shouldered physique. He was on the phone with the president, speaking long-distance to Washington D.C. over a secure line in the U.S. embassy office he'd ascended to after setting into motion the investigation that had led to Carl Ryan's fall from grace. "I know he's out there, just licking his chops for a chance at me."

They were talking about Carl Ryan. The president had assured Gardner that tracking down his fugitive predecessor was being given top priority. Without going into detail, he'd confirmed that the covert operatives involved in thwarting the assassination attempt on Noordin Zailik had been dispatched to Banda Aceh specifically to search for Ryan. The president had additionally arranged for a Delta Force squad to be diverted from work in the Philippines to help with security in Jakarta, not only in the face of any potential threat posed by Ryan, but also to deal with the forces of Jemaah Islamiyah. Even with the measures being taken, however, Gardner had been advised to observe the embassy lockdown and lie low for the time being. It was advice Gardner had every intention of following.

Once the call was over, Gardner felt far less relieved than he'd hoped to after speaking with the president. Yes, Washington was making all the right moves on his behalf, and yet he remained unsettled. He'd had the feeling ever since learning that Ryan had violated his parole and fled the U.S., and the unease had only increased after the incident with Zailik. The president could send all the special ops and Delta Force teams he wanted, but Gardner knew if someone was intent on taking him out, there were always ways to get around the most stringent security measures.

Resigned to the fact that he was now, in effect, as imprisoned inside the embassy as Carl Ryan had been during the months he was behind bars, Gardner decided he might as well make the most of things and catch up on some work. And of that there was plenty.

The trouble in Aceh Province was but one serving on his overloaded plate. There was similar unrest in East Timor and at least a dozen other areas throughout the sprawling archipelago, nearly all of it drummed up by separatist groups looking to splinter off from Indonesia. And, difficult as it was to safeguard American interests while dealing with a centralized government located in Jakarta, the idea of having to contend with heads of state from a handful of newly created countries seemed like a recipe for disaster, not only for the U.S., but also Indonesia itself and all its sister nations spread throughout this watery corner of the world.

While he'd been on the phone, one of Gardner's aides had dropped off a fresh ream of paperwork, most of it dispatches from various consulates spread across the region. He sifted through the documents, looking to see if any of them demanded his immediate attention.

The first important item he came across was an e-mail printout from the consulate in Medan, where a tourist had reported seeing a transient American man being zapped with a stun gun and hauled off to a waiting van by a three men described as being locals. There was no word of a possible motive, and as yet there had been no ransom demands to suggest the abduction was a kidnapping.

The matter sounded mildly intriguing, but Gardner set the e-mail aside. He knew he was being callous, but somehow, in terms of the big picture, the plight of some American beach bum hardly struck him as a priority issue.

14

Gapang, Weh Island

The transient's name was Sandy Whitaker. He'd come to Indonesia four years earlier as an idealistic Baptist missionary, determined to assist his fellow man and spread the word of Christ throughout Sumatra. His first year on the island, the tsunami flattened the mission in Banda Aceh where he was stationed, killing most of the close friends he'd come to Indonesia with. He'd relocated down the coast to Medan, where, a year later, his newfound mission was burned to the ground by Muslim fanatics. By then disillusionment had taken up residence in Whitaker's soul, and a cancer diagnosis six months later had laid to waste what little remained of the man's shredded faith. Chemotherapy managed to keep the cancer in check but had cost Whitaker fifty pounds and all his hair. Bald, emaciated and gripped by dour fatalism, the missionary had walked away from his calling and taken to living off the streets of the Sumatran capital, spending his nights in shelters or at a local park frequented by other Americans whose lives had similarly turned sour.

While panhandling in Medan's shopping district Whitaker was approached by three men, incapacitated and dragged into a waiting van, where one of the men injected him with enough tranquilizers to render him unconscious for the trip to Weh Island.

When he came to, hours later, Whitaker found himself

lying on his side, bound and gagged on the dirt floor of a musty-smelling hut used for storage by Hoa Mursneh's covert militia. The door was open, flooding the enclosure with enough light for Whitaker to make out stacked sacks of rice, several five-gallon plastic jugs of drinking water and a workbench piled with assault rifles and ammunition crates. A guard sat near the doorway, idly cleaning his Ruger automatic. When Whitaker struggled to sit up and tried to shout through the duct tape covering his mouth, the guard glanced at him briefly, then turned back to his gun.

Whitaker remained on the ground, queasy, breathing as best he could through his nose.

A shadow appeared in the doorway. Carl Ryan was backlit so that he appeared in silhouette, preventing Whitaker from noting how closely Ryan resembled him.

From his vantage point, however, Ryan could easily see the likeness.

"He'll do," Ryan said, more to himself than the guard.

With Ryan was one of Anhi Hasbrok's GAM militiamen. Ryan jotted down his clothing measurements. He handed the slip of paper to the soldier and said, "Go to the village and buy two sets of identical clothes. You'll probably have to get something new, so wash the shirts and pants, then scuff the shoes a little. And don't draw any more attention to yourself than you have to."

Whitaker overheard the exchange but had no idea what it meant. When he tried to call out to Ryan, the former ambassador ignored him and walked away from the hut. Whitaker fell silent once more, slumping on the ground in despair.

The guard looked at him and offered a few words that Whitaker felt were intended as something other than consolation.

"You should be excited," the guard said. "You're going to be on television."

Stony Man Farm

HAL BROGNOLA LOOKED AROUND the room. Barbara Price was there along with the full cybernetics team: Aaron Kurtzman, Akira Tokaido, Carmen Delahunt and Huntington Wethers. They all looked exhausted. Brognola suspected they'd been skipping breaks; a sign they had either made some important breakthroughs or were trying to power their way through an impasse.

Once he had their attention, the big Fed quickly passed along the president's decision to deploy Delta forces and additional marines to safeguard the embassy in Jakarta, thereby reducing the chances that Mack Bolan would be further sidetracked from the search for Carl Ryan.

"Good," Kurtzman said, "because we're making progress and there's a lot for our boys to follow up on."

"Let's have it," Brognola said.

There was much to report. The wife of the pilot who'd flown Carl Ryan from Malaysia to Weh Island had just filed a missing persons report. A thorough background check had shown the pilot to be clean, so authorities were concerned the man had fallen victim to foul play, no doubt at Ryan's hand. Kurtzman had put a call through to the National Security Agency, requesting a tweak in the orbital path of spy satellites monitoring Indonesia. Soon they would have extensive sat-cam footage of Weh Island and could check for airfields in hopes of spotting the missing pilot's plane.

As for unearthing clues at the Maryland prison where the former ambassador had done his time, interviews with other inmates had led to naught. The way they told it, Ryan had kept to himself for the most part, rarely engaging others in conversation and taking no one into his confidence. He'd spent countless hours on the prison computers, and both Wethers and Delahunt had analyzed the downloaded entries, the bulk of which showed Ryan had regularly tracked current events throughout Indonesia, with a decided focus on Jakarta and Aceh Province. Prison officials had figured it was merely a habitual interest carried over from his ambassadorial tenure, and while Wethers and Delahunt suspected there might be more to it, they'd found nothing to suggest Ryan was using the Internet specifically to help plot a vendetta against his successor.

"No surprise there," Brognola said. "He had to know he was being monitored. Most likely he just went through entries and read between the lines to learn what he wanted."

Delahunt nodded in agreement, adding, "Unfortunately, short of tracking him down and wringing a confession out of him, there's no way to figure out what was going through his head when he was Web surfing. I tried running some of his entries through an intuitive logic program but no bells or whistles went off."

"Nothing on the missing tsunami funds, either?" Brognola asked.

Delahunt and Wethers shook their heads.

"Fortunately," Kurtzman interjected, "it hasn't been all dead ends. We're making headway elsewhere."

"I'm always in the mood for good news," Brognola said.

"Well, at this point," Barbara Price cautioned, "the news is only promising."

Kurtzman quickly updated Brognola on the altercation at the hunting cabin in Banda Aceh. When he got to the part about the evidence Bolan and the others had come across, he turned things over to Akira Tokaido.

"First, the matchbook," the cyber-wiz reported. "It's from the same hotel on Weh Island where Anhi Hasbrok held a press conference a few hours before all the trouble on the mainland."

"Hasbrok?" Brognola frowned. "What does he have to do with this?"

"Plenty, most likely," Tokaido said. "I took the descriptions

Striker gave of the guys killed near the cabin and cooked up Identi-Kit mug shots, then ran them through the databases. Two guys popped up as former members of the Free Aceh Movement militia."

"Hasbrok's last gig before he went legit," Brognola said.

"Righto," Tokaido replied.

"It's no leap to think guys like that would end up in the private security sector, though, right?" Brognola reasoned.

"No," Price interjected, "but the thing is, this outfit they supposedly belonged to, Indo-Tech Private Security Services…it doesn't exist."

"Forged IDs," Brognola said.

Tokaido nodded. "Hasbrok supposedly disbanded GAM's military arm once he was politically recognized, but it's no stretch to figure he kept a few guys on the sly."

"I suppose not," Brognola said. "But why did he have men looking for Ti Vohn and this Wilki fellow?"

Tokaido shrugged. "Hopefully we'll get a chance to ask him at some point."

"And as far as Vohn and Wilki go," Price said, "we're on their trail."

Price deferred to Delahunt, who apprised Brognola on what they'd come up with pursuing the leads linked to the missing pages from the phone book.

"We've got two different cabbies who gave rides to Wilki and Vohn," Delahunt said. "The first one took them to an Internet café on the main road leading from Banda Aceh to the cabin. They were there an hour then caught another ride to a marina on the outskirts of the city."

"We're requisitioning a tap on the computer they used at the café," Kurtzman added. "Once we get it, we should have something to pass along to Striker so he'll know what to look for when he goes to the marina."

Brognola took in all the information and, like the others,

found reason for guarded optimism. Still, he shared Price's concern that they were still a long way from cracking open the champagne.

"I just wish more of this pointed to Ryan somehow," he thought aloud.

"We're getting there," Kurtzman replied. "Trust me, another break or two and I think we'll find out that all roads lead to Ryan...."

Gapang, Weh Island

CARL RYAN STOPPED at his rental car for his computer and a manila folder thick with documents and paperwork. It would be a couple of hours before everything was ready for him to stage his mock execution. He'd decided to put the time to good use.

The base headquarters for Anhi Hasbrok's Weh Island command post was a large, weathered house trailer concealed from aerial view by several tall, leafy acacia trees. When Ryan entered the trailer, Hasbrok was seated near the eating area, feet propped on an unused chair, can of beer in one hand. He was fouling the air with one of his cigarillos as he stared at his cell phone and a high-powered radio transceiver that were sitting on the kitchen counter.

"That guy'll work," Ryan said. "Is the video equipment ready?"

"It's coming," Hasbrok replied.

"Still no word from Mursneh?" Ryan asked as he set the computer down on a cluttered desk set against the wall behind Hasbrok.

Hasbrok shook his head. "He just missed his second check-in."

"Could be he's in the middle of something," Ryan suggested.

"Maybe so," Hasbrok said, without much conviction.

Ryan opened his computer. While it was booting up, he

took some paperwork from the manila folder and began to spread it out on the desktop.

"Instead of twiddling our thumbs," he told Hasbrok, "I thought we'd go over the plans for Jakarta."

Hasbrok swilled the last of his beer, then stuffed his cigarillo into the can and set it aside. He eyed Ryan impatiently.

"How about we get all this other shit taken care of first?" he suggested.

"That's all out of our hands for the moment," Ryan said. He pointed at the documents now strewn across the desk. "All this needs working out. Preparation…"

"Really?" Hasbrok said. "That part hadn't occurred to me."

Ryan glared at the other man. "Sarcasm won't help us."

"Listen to me, my friend," Hasbrok replied, his voice turning cold. "You want to breach security around the embassy in Jakarta, then kill Gardner and as many others as you can manage. I understand that. I also understand it will be a logistical nightmare with only a limited chance of success. If you want my help upping the odds in your favor, fine, but it's going to have to be on my terms. And my terms are this—we deal with what's in front of us and make sure everything goes off without a hitch, *then* we can move on and work out a plan for Jakarta. Not before."

"And sitting around on your ass is your definition of dealing with what's in front of you?" Ryan countered evenly.

"I'm weighing my options in case Mursneh's run into trouble," Hasbrok said. "I'm thinking through the best strategy for getting back the sympathy votes that bastard Zailik's taking away from me for doing nothing but survive an attempt to send him off on a one-way visit to Allah. I'm thinking of ways to keep my campaign coffers from drying up when I'll most need them. All while I'm sitting on my ass. Do you want me to go on?"

Ryan could see from the look in Hasbrok's eyes that he'd

pushed too hard. Much as he wanted to point out that the other man should be capable enough at multitasking to lend him a hand, he knew it was more important to diffuse the tension between them rather than escalate it. He decided to blink first.

"All right, all right," he told Hasbrok, testing a backhanded apology. "It's just that I've been sitting on this plan for so long, I'm anxious to see it played out. Maybe a little too anxious."

The ploy worked. Appeased, Hasbrok's features softened and he relaxed in his chair.

"I understand," he said, accepting Ryan's olive branch. "And, not to worry. When the time is right, you'll have your vengeance, and if you wait for the right time, you might actually stay around to enjoy it."

"Fair enough," Ryan said. "I'll work out what details I can on my own. Maybe by the time you're ready to join in, things will be in place and we'll be able to move quickly."

"Now you're talking," Hasbrok said.

And so the two men fell to their separate tasks—Ryan scheming, Hasbrok waiting, neither of them particularly satisfied with what had been decided, both of them wishing there was some way they could be rid of the other without jeopardizing what was most important to them.

For his part, Hasbrok found himself wishing that when the time came to stage the fugitive's execution, it would be Ryan rather than his double who wound up dead. Of course, the notion was mere whimsy so long as the bastard continued to sit on the secret as to where he was hiding his ill-gotten fortune.

As he lit another cigarillo, Hasbrok glared at Ryan, who was now immersed in work at his computer, fingers racing across the keyboard, the images on the screen before him changing with each click of the cursor.

"Do you have to smoke that thing in here?" Ryan said, waving away the smoke that had wafted toward him.

Hasbrok said nothing. He took another drag, then blew more smoke as he silently rose from his chair and walked outside.

Long shadows stretched across the grounds. Twilight was moving in. Soon it would be dark. By nightfall, all of his team leaders save for Hoa Mursneh would be back with their sleeper cells throughout the islands, passing along word that every soldier in the dormant militia was to begin reporting daily for extended drills, effective immediately.

Hasbrok hadn't given a reason for demanding the increased preparation, and his men had wisely chosen not to ask for one. He knew he had to be ready to mobilize should he lose the election and decide to attempt a coup.

But that could wait. For now, Hasbrok's concerns remained more immediate. He had no control over determining Mursneh's whereabouts, so he did his best to remain focused on the matter of tracking down Ryan's hidden plunder.

He let his mind wander, hoping it might lead him to the answers he sought. He'd already come to the conclusion that the ambassador's concealed millions were likely somewhere on the island. Given that Ryan's grand scheme involved matters in Jakarta, a thousand miles away, why else would he have come here instead of setting up residence someplace closer to the embassy? Twice already, Hasbrok had arranged for his men to break in to Ryan's beachfront condo while he was away, but they'd found nothing of consequence, so the plunder had to be somewhere else.

A crow fluttered down from the sky and landed on of the outer branch of a lemon tree. The branch sagged beneath its weight, and as the bird squawked, an overripe lemon shook free and splashed into a nearby pond. Hasbrok watched it sink, disappearing from view despite its bright yellow coloring.

Hasbrok found himself mesmerized. He bared his teeth in a joyous smile. He'd just figured out where Ryan had hidden his loot.

15

Banda Aceh

"That's one tangled web," Shelby Ferstera said after the Executioner had brought him up to date, echoing much of the information his colleagues were discussing half a world away at Stony Man Farm.

The two men were in the post-op recovery ward at Banda Aceh's City Hospital. Ferstera's shoulder wound had been cleaned out and sutured and his arm was in a sling. He was slated to remain overnight at the hospital for observation, but the prognosis was good. He'd recover with a full range of motion provided he followed a prescribed regimen of rest and rehabilitation. So far, thanks to the painkillers still streaming through his system, it had been easy enough for him to follow his doctor's orders. Groggy and light-headed, it was all he could do to hold up his end of the conversation with Bolan.

"Must be the meds scrambling my signals a little," he told Bolan, "because I can't figure out why Hasbrok sent men looking for Wilki and Vohn. He has no stake in JI's business as far as I can see."

"Could be political," Bolan speculated. "If he gets credit for helping take down some people linked to the attack on Zailik, it'll mean good press."

"Which is something he could use with that hotshot reporter slinging mud about his militia background," Ferstera said, referring to a television news segment he'd seen earlier in the recovery room.

"Hasbrok dropped off the radar after clashing with that reporter," Bolan said. "My guess is he's still on the island somewhere."

"Sounds like your people think Ryan's hiding out there, too," Ferstera said. "Might be worth checking out. Wouldn't surprise me if you caught 'em both together."

"I might do that," Bolan said. "First I want to follow up on this marina Wilki and Vohn went to after they left the cabin."

"While you do that," Ferstera said, "I'm going to sleep off these painkillers, then drop by the police station and see if I can't get a lead on who leaked that contact list."

"What's your take on the police chief?" Bolan asked.

"Alkihn? It wasn't him," Ferstera insisted. "I've worked with him for years. He's clean."

"If that's the case," Bolan said, "you might want to let him in on what we found at the cabin. Make of the cars, the radio equipment, forged IDs…see if he can run a check."

"Will do, mate," Ferstera promised.

The men were interrupted when someone rapped their knuckles on the door. It was Muhtar Yeilam. The motorcycle policeman was on crutches, dressed in street clothes, his face bandaged.

"They told me I could find you here," he said.

"I'm sorry about your brother," Bolan told the man.

"Our condolences," Ferstera echoed. "That was a brave thing he did. He probably saved the governor's life."

"I was just at his funeral," Yeilam said, hobbling into the room. "I vowed on his grave that I'd help find the people responsible."

"We'll get them," Bolan promised him.

"I want to help," the cop persisted. He turned to Ferstera. "I want to join Densus 88."

"Yes, you told me," Ferstera reminded the younger man.

"I've already cleared it with Chief Alkihn," he said. "He's willing to grant me a leave of absence."

"You need that anyway to recover," Ferstera said. "Your leg…"

"My leg is fine." To illustrate, he cleared his weight off the crutches and leaned them against Ferstera's bed. When he took a few tentative steps, Bolan could see that the man was struggling not to grimace.

"There's a difference between walking a few steps and going into combat where people's lives are on the line," Ferstera told him gently. "I'm sorry, but until you're well enough to—"

"What about you?" Yeilam interrupted. "With all the men you lost, are you going to be content to sit on the sidelines until your shoulder is completely healed?"

Ferstera and Bolan exchanged a glance. By way of response, the Executioner offered a nod of his head. He knew the young cop had just won the argument. Ferstera feigned anger with Bolan then looked at Yeilam.

"I have some funerals of my own to attend before I regroup my men," he said. Grinning slightly, he went on, "In the meantime, I could use somebody to act as liaison with my American colleagues. As a matter of fact, my friend Cooper here was just telling me how much he empathized with your situation."

"I'll do whatever it takes," Yeilam said without hesitation.

Bolan didn't much like the arrangement. His preference was to work alone, and it was enough that he'd brought along Kissinger and Grimaldi for backup. But he knew and understood the gleam of determination in Muhtar Yeilam's eyes. If the man wasn't brought into the fold, the odds were he'd try to go after Jemaah Islamiyah on his own, a situation that more than likely would turn out badly for all concerned. Bolan suspected that his mission would be less compromised if Yeilam were kept on a leash so that he could keep an eye on him.

"I have some leads to follow up on," the Executioner told the Indonesian cop. "I could use an interpreter…."

Java Sea

VOHN FIGURED IT was almost time.

She and Wilki had been back out on the water for nearly an hour. She'd spent most of that time belowdecks in the bunk quarters, pretending to sleep. The only pills she'd taken, however, had been the ones to combat seasickness. They'd worked, thankfully, and the faint ache in her stomach was merely from having overeaten back in Marunda. She was wide awake, filled with nervous energy.

She forced herself to lie in bed a few minutes longer, listening to the steady drone of the boat's engines and staring out the portal as the last of the day's light drained from the sky. She thought about what she'd learned at the helm with Wilki after they'd pulled out from the dock. She'd gently probed Wilki for details on how to operate the boat, phrasing her questions in a way intended to make her appear more naive than inquisitive, and the ploy had seemed to work. Like most men she knew, Wilki took an insipid pride in flaunting an understanding of mechanical issues that seemed beyond the grasp of women, and he'd seemed to have taken perverse pleasure in having to explain things that, for him, were rudimentary. She had played along, stroking his ego and playing dumb, all the while committing to memory everything she'd need to know once she took over the controls. It had all gone so smoothly that now, in retrospect, Vohn wondered if perhaps she had overplayed her hand. What if Wilki had sensed something was amiss and merely indulged her, stringing her along until he'd been able to figure out what she was up to?

Stop being paranoid, she told herself. Of course she'd fooled him. If she hadn't, he would have called her on it.

She knew she was getting cold feet, looking for excuses not to follow through on her plan. But she fought off the feeling, reminding herself what was at stake. If she didn't stick with her plan, by morning she'd be turned over to Agmed Hasem. There was no way she would let that happen.

Once the room was dark, she got out of bed and dressed hurriedly before turning on the light. She'd found a ballpoint pen earlier while going through the drawers. She quickly disassembled it, keeping the plastic outer tube. Once she'd plugged the tip with paper, she took out the sleeping pills. One by one, she opened the gelatin capsules and poured the powder into the pen's outer casing. After six capsules, the tube was almost completely filled. She figured that would be enough. She wadded more paper into the top opening, then concealed the makeshift dispenser in the palm of her hand.

When she emerged from the sleeping quarters, Wilki was where she'd left him, standing at the controls, eyes on the dark water before him. Hearing her, he turned slightly.

"That wasn't long," he said.

"I thought half a sleeping pill would be enough," she lied. "Apparently not."

"We still have a long way to go."

"I know. I was just getting some water," she said. "Do you want anything?"

"Another energy drink," Wilki told her, just as she hoped he would. "Maybe a couple while you're at it."

She went to the galley. By the time she'd reached the refrigerator she'd already unsealed the top of the pen. She took one of the energy drinks out and popped the tab, then quickly poured in the sleeping powder. She stirred the liquid then discarded the pen half and grabbed a second drink from the refrigerator. She returned to the helm, pretending to take a sip from the opened can. For Wilki's benefit, she made a face as she held the drinks out.

"How can you drink that stuff?!" she complained. "It tastes like cleaning fluid!"

Wilki laughed and, again, as she had hoped, he quickly guzzled the drink in one long boastful gulp, then smacked his lips and cracked open the second can. He grinned at her as if he'd just performed the world's most Herculean task.

"You men," Ti Vohn teased. "I'll never understand you."

Wilki grinned, taking it as a compliment. "Go back to sleep," he told her. "Next thing you know, we'll be there."

Vohn nodded and smiled demurely. *That's what you think.*

ASIDE FROM THE CHANGE from day to night, the marina looked much the same as it had when Dihb Wilki and Ti Vohn had come by earlier in the day. The old car was still parked just off the street and the scooter remained propped against the side wall of the bait and tackle shop on the docks. There was a light on inside the shanty, and after the Executioner knocked a second time on the weathered door, it was finally answered by an elderly man with a scraggly beard and large-framed wire-rimmed glasses.

Muhtar Yeilam was with Bolan. He spoke briefly with the older man, asking the questions Bolan had fed him on the drive from the hospital. Once they were finished, the man took a step back and closed the door, throwing a dead bolt.

"He says the car belongs to boat's owner," Yeilam told Bolan, referring to the cabin cruiser depicted on what had been—according to Aaron Kurtzman's long-distance hard-drive scan—the last Web site Dihb Wilki had accessed while using one of the computers at the Internet café located five miles down the road.

"He was watching through the shutters when a man and a woman boarded the boat along with the owner."

"Wilki and Vohn?" Bolan asked.

"Sounds like it," Yeilam said. "He says the owner's been trying to sell the boat for weeks. He figured they were just taking it out for a test ride, but they never came back."

"Something tells me they never will," Bolan said.

"You think they stole the boat?"

Bolan nodded. The news hadn't taken him by surprise. All the evidence had already pointed to the likelihood that Wilki had targeted the boat as a getaway vehicle. Now it seemed a lock.

Bolan and Yeilam left the dock, passing the boat owner's car. Jack Grimaldi was behind the wheel of a replacement SUV and John Kissinger was sitting up front next to him, his face bathed in the bluish glow of the computer on his lap. Bolan and Yeilam got in back, then the Executioner quickly passed along what they'd learned from the man in the shack.

"Alrighty, then," Grimaldi said. "Now that we know what we're looking for, all we have to do is figure out which way they went."

"They headed west when they set out," Yeilam said. "There's nothing out there, so they probably turned south at some point and headed down the coast."

"It's not much, but we'll go with that," Bolan said. He turned to Kissinger. "Check with the Farm and see if they can check the sat-cams. Hopefully the boat will show up on one of—"

"Hang on," Kissinger cut in, holding up a hand to silence Bolan. His attention was still focused on the laptop screen. He apologized for the interruption, then went on, "Speaking of sat-cams, the Farm ran a fine-toothed comb over all the footage taken of Weh Island today."

"They found the missing plane?" Bolan asked.

"No, but they might've found something even better," Kissinger replied. "They got a read on some kind of camp half-hidden in the trees at the base of the volcano there. It's also less than an hour's drive from that hotel where Hasbrok spoke earlier today."

"Same hotel as the one on the matchbook," Bolan said.

"That's the one," Kissinger confirmed. "If we're going on the theory that Hasbrok's retained some of his militia, this camp's probably as good a place as any to start looking for them."

"Definitely worth a shot," Grimaldi said.

"Agreed," Bolan said. "But it doesn't look like that's where Wilki and Vohn were headed, and I don't want to let that trail get any colder."

"We can split up," Kissinger suggested.

Bolan thought it over, then said, "Let's do it. But first let's see what we can do about getting our hands on a helicopter...."

Java Sea

DIHB WILKI YAWNED, fighting off the sudden weariness that had come over him. He didn't understand it. Energy drinks usually perked him up in the face of fatigue. Yet here he was, barely able to stand at the controls, his legs feeling like lead, his brain fogging.

Then, in a flash, it came to him.

"That bitch!" he seethed, cutting back on the boat's throttle. She'd done this to him.

Wilki felt drunk as he staggered from the helm. By the time he reached the door, he was on his knees, clutching at the frame to keep from falling completely to the floor. The sleeping quarters were only a few yards away, but as his strength ebbed, the distance seemed insurmountable. Instead he crawled to the bathroom and knelt with his face poised over the toilet. He had to clear his system and get rid of whatever she put into his drink.

The ferret-eyed informant slackened his jaw and thrust a finger deep into his throat. He gagged and brought up half-digested bits of beef satay. The sedatives, however, had already been absorbed into his system, and the vomiting only made him weaker. When he fumbled at his waistband, groping for his pistol, his other hand slipped free of the toilet's rim and he went down hard, groaning as his face struck the floor tiles. The tiles were cold but felt comforting.

"Bitch," Wilki murmured, barely able to get the word out.

He wavered between sleep and consciousness, his train of thought constantly derailed in his failing attempt to stay awake. When he heard Vohn emerge from the sleeping quarters and make her way to the bathroom, it was all he could do to turn his head and get a look at her.

"You seem tired," she told him, a cold smile playing across her lips. "Maybe it would be best if you let me take over."

Wilki still had the gun in his hand, but it felt as if it weighed as much as the boat itself. He was powerless to prevent the woman from taking it from him and pointing the barrel at his face.

"Pleasant dreams," she said as she pulled the trigger.

16

Gapang, Weh Island

Carl Ryan was ready for his execution.

He paced the converted barracks, where bunks had been cleared to one side near the bare wall where a single chair had been placed. With him in the large room were a handful of soldiers. Two carried black hoods and loaded carbines, another held a lethal-looking scimitar. The man with the sword was looking over a sheet of paper where Ryan had written the lines the swordbearer was to deliver once the camera was rolling. A fourth soldier sat on one of the bunks, adjusting the light fixture mounted to a video camera resting on his lap.

Ryan had written a statement for him to read as well. He looked it over, making a few last-minute changes. He was wearing the new clothes that had been purchased in the village a few hours earlier. The shirt's creases had been washed out and, as he'd requested, the shoes had been scuffed. Everything seemed in order.

Ryan was surprised that Hasbrok had opted not to attend the mock execution, deciding instead to go to Banda Aceh to check on the whereabouts of Hoa Mursneh and the other men who'd gone missing while looking for Dihb Wilki and Ti Vohn. He understood Hasbrok's need to tend to his own priorities, but Ryan thought the GAM strongman could just as easily have remained on the island and monitored the situation with phone calls to Sinso Dujara. It struck Ryan as yet another example of Hasbrok's unwillingness to commit himself adequately to the operation in Jakarta. For the plan to have any chance of succeeding, Hasbrok had to get on board, and quick. Each day they delayed, the greater the likelihood they would find themselves having to contend with increased security at the embassy. Things would be difficult enough as it was.

The main doors to the one-time chapel opened behind Ryan. He turned and saw another two soldiers enter, carrying the limp form of Sandy Whitaker. The man had been sedated again and had been dressed in clothes identical to Ryan's.

"Over here," Ryan directed, gesturing to the floor directly in front of the chair set against the far wall. He followed as Whitaker was carried him over, then pointed again. "Face down, feet toward the chair."

Once Whitaker had been laid out across the floor, Ryan turned his attention to the man brandishing the scimitar. The man's eyes were closed and his lips moved as he silently practiced his lines.

"It'd be better if you didn't just memorize," Ryan told the man. "Just understand the content and say it your own way. It can't sound rehearsed."

The man nodded, but in a way that suggested he didn't trust his ability to ad-lib. Ryan tried not to be overly concerned. After all, they would not be broadcasting live. If there were glitches, it would be easy enough to stop the taping and start over.

Once the cameraman signaled that he was ready, Ryan told everyone to take their positions. As he sat in the chair directly in front of Whitaker, the carbine-wielding soldiers slipped on their black hoods, then took up positions on either side of him. The man with the scimitar donned a hood as well and placed himself in the foreground, facing the camera. The cameraman's free hand was extended out to one side as he peered through the viewfinder, making certain that Whitaker was not in the frame. Satisfied, he signaled for the sword-bearer to begin.

"Jemaah Islamiyah has captured an American dog, praise Allah!" the man with the scimitar shouted, gesturing at Carl Ryan. "Watch as we show you what happens to infidels!"

ANHI HASBROK hadn't gone to Banda Aceh.

He hadn't even left the island.

While Carl Ryan was staging his mock execution at the GAM militia camp, Hasbrok was deep in the dark waters of Gapang Bay, lighting his way with a high-powered flashlight as he roamed the same coral formations Ryan had explored a few days before. Hasbrok had yet to come across what he'd hoped he might find, but he was certain Ryan's pilfered fortune lay hidden somewhere in the depths.

It seemed so obvious he was surprised it hadn't occurred to him before. When Ryan had wanted to go diving soon after his arrival on the island, he'd told Hasbrok that it was the thing that'd he'd missed most while in prison. At the time, the ex-planation had seemed plausible enough that Hasbrok hadn't questioned it. But now he knew better. What Ryan had really wanted to do was make sure that his fortune had remained un-touched during the time he was away. That had to be it.

Of course, knowing where to look for the plunder was proving a challenge. Oblivious to the sea life sharing the water around him, Hasbrok had carefully searched the coral reefs and the irregular formations rising up from them. So far he'd come across the fractured remains of several small boats, bits of encrusted trash and even remnants of a human skeleton, but there had been no submerged locker, no sunken treasure chest, no trace of anything that could even remotely pass for a hiding place.

Hasbrok checked his cylinder readings and realized he was

running out of time. He gave one last cursory inspection to a fistlike formation protruding from the shelf closest to him. The stark beam of his flashlight roused an octopus from under the shelf, limbs at first asprawl, then going rigid as the beast propelled its way clear of the light's beam, leaving in its wake an inky cloud.

Discouraged, the GAM leader made his way back to the anchor line where he'd begun his quest and slowly rose to the surface. He would try again during the day, he decided. Perhaps in better light he would spot something he'd missed.

Once back aboard his cabin cruiser, Hasbrok drew in the anchor, then drearily made his way to the helm, ready to head ashore. He checked his cell phone and saw there was a message from Sinso Dujara. The news was not good. Hoa Mursneh was dead, along with the men he'd taken with him to find Dihb Wilki and Ti Vohn before the Americans. They'd been killed near a cabin where Wilki had supposedly taken Vohn after fleeing the city. The intelligence director wasn't certain, but it looked as if the Americans were responsible for the deaths. There was no word as to whether the two fugitive JI sympathizers had been captured or were still at large.

Hasbrok tried to rein in his growing anger. Why had he let Ryan talk him into sending his men on that fool's errand? Instead of reaping the political windfall that would have come from finding Wilki and Vohn, he had to face the possibility that Mursneh's militia history and that of the other men would come to light. If it came to that, it wouldn't matter what kind of forged credentials they'd been carrying; that bastard reporter Mestra would smell a story and go after it until he blew the lid off Hasbrok's secret retention of military troops.

Fuming, Hasbrok lit a cigarillo, then started up the cruiser's engines. He was about to open the throttles when he suddenly stopped. Through the windshield, inland beyond Ryan's condominium complex, he saw a helicopter hovering.

Alarmed, Hasbrok idled the engines and searched for his binoculars, then headed out onto the deck so that he could get a better look at the chopper. He didn't like what he saw.

Once he brought the binoculars fully into focus, he cursed. "This is the last thing I need!"

SHELBY FERSTERA had been awake when Bolan had called him at the hospital requesting help in securing a helicopter. Thanks to the Australian's clout with the Indonesian military, the Executioner's crew had been given access to a decades-old Huey UH-1V outfitted for medevac duty. The massive bird was larger than what Bolan would have liked for an insertion maneuver, but given the circumstances, he'd decided against wasting time trying to get his hands on something more discreet. With Jack Grimaldi at the controls, the chopper had lifted off within an hour after its requisition and made its way to Weh Island with Muhtar Yeilam riding shotgun and Bolan sharing the passenger compartment with John Kissinger and a pair of infantrymen who'd been assigned to ensure that the warbird was returned in one piece.

Hovering wide of the gaseous plume that trailed up from the irritable bowels of the slumbering volcano, Grimaldi informed Bolan, "No place to touch down. You'll have to use the rope."

"On it," Bolan said.

Anticipating the need, the Executioner had already secured the heavy-gauge line to a floor mount. He was ready for battle as well, his tall, rugged frame straining the seams of his borrowed camo fatigues. An M-16 carbine was slung across his shoulder and his Beretta was secured within a web holster, leaving more room on his ammunition belt for extra magazines and a trio of hand grenades. Kissinger, similarly armed, had already opened the compartment door and was donning a pair of leather gloves to guard against rope burn on the way down. One of the Indonesians had negotiated his way into joining the insertion, offering not only his interpreter skills, but also an expertise with the M-72 LAW he'd brought on-board. Bolan doubted they would be encountering any tanks but figured, in a worst-case scenario, that the extra firepower might come in handy.

Once the rope had been fed out, Kissinger started the exodus. The Indonesian soldier went next. As he waited his turn, Bolan called out to Grimaldi, "Good luck finding that boat."

"We'll need it," Grimaldi replied. "Hope things go smoothly on your end."

Bolan nodded, then dropped from the chopper and lowered himself down the rope. Soon he joined the others on the ash-strewn rim of the volcano. The soldier left behind was just beginning to retrieve the line when the Huey banked away from the crater and drifted off into the night.

"Who cut the cheese?" Kissinger wisecracked, his eyes stinging from the volcano's toxic fumes.

"Hopefully it won't be as bad downhill," Bolan said.

The Executioner led the way, sidestepping to keep from slipping on the thick, powdery layer of grey ash that blanketed the steep slope. The half moon overhead provided enough illumination for the men to see where they were going. After thirty yards they reached a faint ledge, beyond which the mountain's pitch lessened. The ledge was covered with bootprints, none of which extended farther upward or sideways. A well-worn trail led down in a straight line. Judging from the space between the freshest of the tracks, it seemed clear that they had not been made by casual hikers but rather by men jogging up the mountain and back.

"A little out of the way for marathon training," Kissinger surmised.

Bolan nodded. "Boot-camp drills, more likely," he said.

"If that's the case, we're on the right track," Kissinger said.

The path before them was five yards wide. Random tufts

of ankle-high grass were the only vegetation and the scant few
boulders rising up through the ash-draped soil on either side
of the trail offered little in the way of cover, much less protection. Bolan knew they were vulnerable and would remain
so until they reached the bottom of the slope. As they started
downhill, he told Kissinger and the other man to spread out
as best they could. Bolan stayed close to one edge of the trail.
Kissinger, hanging a few yards back, ventured to the other
side, leaving the Indonesian to bring up the rear, dead center
on the trail.

The soft earth cushioned each step but Bolan could still feel
a jarring impact as he navigated the steep slope, staring far
down the hillside. They were halfway to the mountain's base
when, through the trees below, he detected lights, including
what looked to be the front beams of a vehicle heading away
from the volcano. Not certain if the others had seen the lights,
he held a hand out to get their attention, then pointed.

"Looks like they don't have an early curfew," Kissinger
whispered. He unslung his carbine and cradled it into firing
position. Bolan did the same. Heading down the pitched
incline would be more difficult without his hands free, but
with clear signs of activity below, he was more concerned
about being able to defend himself.

The precaution proved well advised, as seconds later the
night's silence was broken by the rattle of an assault rifle. The
fired rounds pummeled the trail just to Bolan's right, stitch-
ing their way toward the Indonesian soldier.

Bolan abandoned the trail, tucking the carbine in close to
his chest as he zigzagged down the uneven slope. The going
was precarious as the ground beneath him was now clotted
with loose stones and small rocks. For each sure step there
would be one where the ground gave way under his weight.
Several times he dropped to one knee, raising welts along his
thigh as he half-fell, half-slid his way downhill, raising a

cloud of volcanic ash and dislodging the loose gravel around him. It was as if he'd become a one-man avalanche.

After another twenty yards, the ground abruptly fell away from Bolan and he was thrown forward, off-balance, into a deep recess. He struck the far edge of the gully knee-first, then with his shoulder, jarring his carbine loose. The rifle sailed past him and rolled sideways another five yards before coming to a rest. Bolan, meanwhile, slumped into the cavity, dazed. He had the presence of mind to drop as low as he could, avoiding the stream of gunfire that, moments later, skimmed past the gully's rim. As he waited for his head to clear, the Executioner reached for his web holster, unsheathing his Beretta. He was down but not out and hoped the same could be said for the others.

KISSINGER WAS HAVING an easier time of it. The Executioner and the soldier had drawn most of the follow-up fire, giving him precious seconds to charge his way downhill. He encountered the same shifting terrain as Bolan and found himself slipping and sliding, but instead of a gully, his divergence from the main trail led him to a raised cleft in the mountain, high enough to provide cover while still letting him continue his way downward without being spotted from below. He made his way slowly so as to disturb the loose ground as little as possible, and once the cleft began to taper off, he stopped.

There was a slight breeze, carrying with it the smell of smoke. It wasn't the sulfur smell of the volcano, but rather that of something burning. As he listened, between gunshots Kissinger could hear the crackle of flames. He wasn't sure what to make of it and he was wary of peering above the cleft to see where the fire was burning.

As he stayed put, weighing his next move, the Stony Man weaponsmith stole a glance over his shoulder. Higher up on the trail, the Indonesian soldier had been hit. He was down, his antitank weapon on the ground beside him. Fortunately, the enemy below had turned his attention from him and was trading fire with the Executioner farther down the slope. Kissinger could see that the soldier was still alive and, seconds later, the Indonesian slowly snaked an arm forward, retrieving the M-71. With what seemed to be an excruciating effort, the man eased himself to a sitting position and propped the LAW to his shoulder, taking aim downhill toward the trees.

Kissinger was anticipating the man's shot when, out of the corner of his eye, he detected motion on the ground a few yards to his left. It was the moon-cast shadow of someone nearing the upper edge of the cleft almost directly above him.

Silently raising his carbine, Kissinger leaned away from the upthrust, eyes on the ledge. Finally he saw him—a man in camo fatigues so focused on drawing a bead on the Indonesian that he didn't realize a closer target was but a few feet below him.

Kissinger had only one option. He triggered an autoburst, riddling the enemy gunner before he could take out the Indonesian soldier. The other man died with a look of bewilderment and plunged forward, lifelessly toppling over the cleft and landing directly next to Kissinger.

Kissinger was helping himself to the man's carbine when the Indonesian fired. Kissinger could hear the LAW's 66 mm HEAT warhead *whoosh* past him into forest at the base of the mountain. An explosion resounded across the mountainside, followed by the crashing of a tall tree brought down by the blast. By the time the tree was down, shaking the ground with the force of its fall, Kissinger was on his feet. He doubted that the soldier had been able to spot any gunners down in the forest. The blast had been intended to create a diversion, and Kissinger was ready to make the most of it. One carbine slung over his shoulder, the other clenched in firing position, he broke from cover and bolted downhill, ready to engage the enemy....

BOLAN HAD TAKEN the cue as well, scrambling up out of his makeshift foxhole, then planting himself long enough to turn his Beretta loose on a gunman who'd been flushed out into the open by the falling tree. The man went down.

Bolan holstered his pistol and scooped up his fallen carbine, then joined Kissinger in storming the last stretch of ground leading to the forest. Through the gap carved out by the M-72 he could see flames eating at a structure just past the trees. Bolan figured it had to be part of the camp and veered in its direction, passing the man he'd just killed.

The two Stony Man warriors converged near the fallen tree, taking cover behind its thick trunk when they were met with more gunfire. Kissinger glanced back up the hill to see if the Indonesian would be joining him. It wasn't to be. Whether he'd been shot again after firing the warhead or had succumbed from his initial wound, he was down, not far from where he'd fired the M-72.

"I think we lost him," Kissinger called out to Bolan.

Bolan nodded grimly, eyes trained on the wooded area between them and the camp. He spotted someone moving toward them, advancing from tree to tree. The Executioner timed his shot and caught the man once he broke from cover.

"Let's make sure he didn't die in vain," Bolan told Kissinger. He signaled for Kissinger to head left, then broke away from the tree and stagger-stepped his way to the forest. He crouched low, using the ferns for camouflage as he advanced toward the camp. When he heard a rustling far off in the woods he swung his carbine around, holding his fire once he realized it was Kissinger. The motion wasn't wasted, however, as he caught glimpse of a sniper lurking in a tree to Kissinger's immediate left.

Bolan strafed the tree. The sniper's rifle dropped to the ground, but his body snagged on one of the branches and was kept aloft, dangling. Kissinger waited to make sure the man was dead, then continued toward the blazing building. Bolan did the same.

They met one final bout of resistance as they cleared the forest and entered the camp, engaging blasts from a gunman poised near the open door of the converted chapel. His shots were off the mark, and a return crossfire from both Bolan and Kissinger sent him reeling back inside.

Finally, for the first time since the initial volley had been fired, the sound of gunfire faded and the only noise emanating through the camp was the crackle of flames engulfing the remains of Hasbrok's camp headquarters. Keeping a wary eye on the other outbuildings, Bolan and Kissinger made their way toward the fire.

"They torched it themselves," Kissinger murmured.

Bolan agreed. "Destroying evidence."

"That's what happens when you don't have a shredder," Kissinger said.

"Let's check around," Bolan replied.

They searched the camp together, starting with a panel truck and a pair of unattended Jeeps, then going from building to building. They encountered no one and came across no more bodies until they reached the chapel. There, after stepping past the last man they'd brought down, they saw, sprawled on the floor near a chair set before the far wall, the corpse of a tanned Caucasian man wearing civilian clothes. He'd been decapitated, and the head lay several yards from the body next to a bloodstained scimitar. The man's head was shaved, his face turned away from Bolan and Kissinger.

"Looks like we're a little late," Kissinger said.

Bolan didn't answer. He strode past the cots and leaned over, picking up a black, woven hood. He carried it with him as he went to take a closer look at the body and its dismembered head.

"Ryan?" Kissinger called out.

Bolan glanced back at Kissinger. "Close…"

17

Much as Carl Ryan wanted to drive without his lights on, the road leading away from the camp was too winding and treacherous to allow it. He compensated by keeping his foot to the accelerator as much as he dared, taking some corners wide, other times cutting in close to the shoulder, trying to put as much distance between his rented Land Rover and the camp as possible. He wondered if it would all be in vain. He had the sunroof open and with each passing second he was certain that he would hear the thunder of a low-flying helicopter or at least detect its searchlight probing through the trees and off the mountainside, seeking him out.

Anhi Hasbrok's warning that the camp was being raided had come just moments after the staged execution. Ryan had felt the taping had gone well, but, in an instant, the whole production had been rendered moot. He had the video camera and the taped footage with him, but unless Hasbrok's men somehow managed to thwart the raid and dispose of the transient's body, it would be discovered. He could upload the taped beheading onto the Internet and get a million hits, but word would get out that it was all a hoax and that it wasn't him but rather an imposter who had been slain. The U.S. government would know he was still alive and they would redouble their efforts to track him down.

Rounding another bend, Ryan came upon an opossum lumbering slowly across the road. He instinctively swerved to avoid it and slammed on the brakes. The car fishtailed. His front end clipped the guardrail protecting motorists from a sheer, thirty-foot drop-off. The railing held but threw the car into a spin. Rubber burned on the asphalt as Ryan swerved back onto the road, now facing the way he'd just come. He pumped the brakes again, finally bringing the car to a stop. The driver's side headlight had been knocked out of commission by the impact with the guardrail. The other beam illuminated the slow-moving creature that had nearly proved Ryan's undoing. The animal had stopped in the road; it stared back at Ryan for a moment before plodding on to the shoulder.

Despite the damage to the front end, the Land Rover still seemed driveable. Ryan backed up carefully, then negotiated a three-point turn, righting his course. He forged on, driving more slowly, still on the alert for any sign of a search helicopter. He'd progressed less than a mile when steam began to rise up from under the hood. The thermometer gauge on the dashboard began to needle into the red. The run-in with the guardrail had clearly damaged one of the engine hoses.

"Damn it!" he roared, pounding the steering wheel in frustration. Could nothing go right for him?

Ryan was headed downhill, so he shifted into Neutral, easing the strain on the engine. Steam continued to billow forth, however, hampering his visibility.

Once he reached the bottom of the incline, the fugitive finally abandoned the road, putting the car back into gear long enough to detour onto a driveway leading to an isolated, two-story cabin set back some fifty yards from the road. There was a pickup truck parked in front and a light shone in one of the downstairs windows.

Ryan pulled off the driveway and parked below the overhanging branches of a tree. When he turned off the engine, he could hear the steam hissing beneath the hood. He ignored it and grabbed the pistol resting next to the video camera on the passenger seat beside him.

Getting out of the Land Rover, he left the door ajar and took long, purposeful strides up the driveway. He was nearing the cabin when the front porch light came on. Ryan quickened his pace and was within a few yards of the porch when he saw a man pull aside the curtain draped across the door's small, decorative window.

Ryan raised his gun and fired twice through the window, shattering the glass. The man fell from view. Ryan bounded up the steps and tried the door. It was locked. He took a step back, fired at the lock, then lunged forward, shouldering his full weight against the door. It gave and he charged into the cabin. The man lay dead on the floor. A woman who looked to be the same age stood several feet away. Her mouth was open but she was too traumatized to scream.

"The keys!" Ryan demanded, pointing the gun at her. "The keys to the truck. Where are they?"

Trembling, the woman looked to her right. Ryan followed her gaze and spotted a set of keys on a counter separating the kitchen from a dining area. He stepped around the man he'd just killed and grabbed the keys, then turned the gun back on the woman and fired, striking her in the chest. As she crumpled to the hardwood floor, Ryan looked around, gun held out before him, ready to kill anyone else who dared show themselves. When no one appeared, he left the cabin and started the truck. He drove to his car, then idled the engine and got out long enough to retrieve the video camera.

Once he was back on the road, Ryan headed toward the village. He wasn't sure of his next move, but he knew his best chance of eluding capture was to find a way off the island as quickly as possible. His condo was on the other side of the village. If he could make it there and get to his boat, he could...

"Boat," Ryan muttered aloud, a realization coming to him.

For the first time since receiving Hasbrok's frantic call, Ryan found himself wondering how the GAM leader could have spotted a helicopter dropping men off at the top of the volcano if he was all the way across the strait in Banda Aceh? It wasn't possible. He had to have been closer. What was more, given the island's topography and the density of the forests that surrounded the mountain, there was no place in all of Weh where one could even see the volcano's peak. To have that view, one had to be out on the water; specifically out in the middle of Gapang Bay, near the submerged coral reefs where Ryan had concealed the waterproof container holding the tsunami plunder he'd converted on the black market into five million dollars worth of uncut diamonds.

"You son of a bitch!" Ryan seethed, flooring the truck's accelerator and racing along the road that circumvented the village and led to the bay. He could only hope that he wasn't too late.

Banda Aceh

CARL RYAN WOULDN'T FIND Anhi Hasbrok once he reached Gapang Bay.

The GAM strongman, already fearing the worst for his militia camp on Weh Island, had navigated his boat clear of the bay and circled across the channel to Banda Aceh. He'd put a call through to Sinso Dujara, and the intelligence director was waiting for him when he pulled his cabin cruiser into the newest of Banda Aceh's marinas on the city's eastern shore. Most of the slips were occupied, some by houseboats whose occupants were out on the decks enjoying the warm night, but at this late hour the dock itself was otherwise deserted.

"Yes, the camp was raided," Dujara confirmed once the cabin cruiser had docked and he'd help Hasbrok disembark. The older man kept his voice low as they made their way past the houseboats. "It was the Americans, as you suspected."

As they headed for the parking lot, Hasbrok, hair still damp from his fruitless scuba search, hurled some choice epithets at the mysterious covert operatives who had become a scourge to him. Dujara let the other man vent, casually glancing about the marina. Up in an enclosed two-story observation tower, a security guard was on duty, casing out his domain with bored diligence. There was little for him to monitor. Aside from Dujara, Hasbrok and those aboard the houseboats, there were only a few couples scattered along the beachfront walkway adjacent to the marina.

Once Hasbrok's tirade had run its course, Dujara quickly filled him in on the rest of the details. After receiving Hasbrok's call, he'd contacted the Weh Island police force, directing them to the camp based on an "anonymous" tip. By the time they'd arrived, Hasbrok's men had been routed and his headquarters had burned to the ground.

"I assume the latter was your idea," the intelligence director said, wrapping up.

Hasbrok nodded. "There was information there that could have linked me to the camp," he said.

"Some of your men could have provided the same information under interrogation," Dujara said. "So I would suppose it's to your benefit they were all killed."

"What about Ryan?" Hasbrok asked once the men reached Dujara's government-owned car. "Did they get him, too?"

"Apparently not," Dujara conceded. "Only the stand-in he had executed in his place."

"A lot of good that did him," Hasbrok said. The gubernatorial candidate's temper flared anew. He cursed Ryan with a few vile names he hadn't gotten around to calling the Americans, concluding, "Since he set foot back on the islands, he's brought me nothing but bad luck and headaches."

Dujara pulled out of the parking lot and headed down a long, two-lane access road leading to the main highway linking the marina with the city.

"Speaking of fortunes," the intelligence director said, "I

take it you weren't able to find out where he's keeping his take from the tsunami funds."

"No," Hasbrok replied bitterly, steering clear of the truth. "Not a thing."

"That's unfortunate," Dujara said, slowing the car. By the time he'd pulled off to the shoulder and brought the car to a sudden stop, he'd drawn a handgun with a three-inch silencer from the holster beneath his suit coat. Hasbrok, taken by surprise, had no time to react before three close-range, muffled rounds pounded the life from him. He slumped forward, bleeding onto the leather upholstery, his seat belt keeping him from falling to the floor.

"You've become a liability to me, my friend," Dujara murmured, mimicking his slain comrade's familiar affectation. "I hope you understand it was nothing personal."

18

Banda Aceh, Indonesia

Shelby Ferstera managed a few hours of sleep before checking himself out of the hospital. It was now well into the night. Unable to drive with his arm in a sling, he flagged down a motorized trishaw and asked the driver to take him to police headquarters. He'd already roused Irwandi Alkihn from his sleep and convinced the police chief to meet him there. Ferstera had until morning before the scheduled flight that would take him to Medan for the first two funerals for his fallen colleagues; in that time he hoped, with Alkihn's help, to be able to smoke out the mole in the police department who'd leaked the list of Dihb Wilki's contacts to the goon squad Ferstera and the Americans had run up against near the hunting cabin. Ferstera had the list with him, along with the incriminating matchbook and the falsified identification papers taken from the men killed in the altercation.

THE POLICE CHIEF ARRIVED at the station apologizing for being late and, moments later, Ferstera was behind closed doors in Alkihn's office, ready to discuss his theories.

"We can get into that in a moment," the police chief told Ferstera, "but first I need to bring you up to date on a few things."

Ferstera wasn't surprised. "I figured you were late getting here for a reason."

"Several reasons, actually," the police chief said.

Alkihn explained that following his phone conversation with Ferstera, the police chief had received, in quick succession, two additional distress calls. The first had been from Weh Island, where, Ferstera learned, the insertion probe undertaken by his American counterparts had turned into a full-scale conflagration. The Americans had come through the battle unscathed, but an Indonesian soldier accompanying them was among the fatalities, which included at least seven men whose identities had yet to be determined.

"They're Hasbrok's men, though, right?" Ferstera said. "Former members of his militia."

The police chief's eyes narrowed. "How did you know that?"

"Just piecing things together," Ferstera said. "It's the only explanation that makes sense."

"Perhaps to you," Alkihn responded. "But they were prepared to make it look otherwise."

"What do you mean?"

The police chief told Ferstera about the decapitated body found in the camp's converted chapel along with a scimitar and black hoods identical to those worn by Jemaah Islamiyah in previous incidents involving the beheading of kidnap victims. In this particular incident, the victim bore a striking resemblance to former U.S. ambassador Carl Ryan. Alkihn seemed of the opinion that the resemblance was more than coincidental.

"They'd apparently just staged the execution when all hell broke loose," the police chief reported. "It stands to reason they taped it, for whatever reason, but we haven't been able to find the camera. Or Ryan, either, for that matter. I'm sending more men to help your colleagues search for him."

"You're certain Ryan is involved?" Ferstera asked.

"That's what I've been told," Alkihn said.

"By whom?"

"Sinso Dujara," Alkihn said. "I'd just gotten off the phone with my contacts on Weh Island when he called."

"He was there, too?" Ferstera asked.

"No, he was calling from the mainland," Alkihn said. "I don't have all the details yet, but apparently he'd been working overtime on those murders in Gunung Leuser when he came across evidence that Hasbrok may have had a hand in it."

"Bloody convenient, eh?" Ferstera said. "I'm surprised it took him that long."

"I'm not sure I follow you," Alkihn said.

"C'mon, mate," Ferstera replied. "Dujara is the governor's pet bloodhound, right? Zailik wanted that whole mess dropped on somebody else's doorstep besides his. What better scapegoat than the bloke running against him?"

"If you're saying Zailik ordered a frame-up, I think you're off the mark," Alkihn said.

"What makes you so sure?" Ferstera asked.

"The way Dujara explained it on the phone, once he came up with this lead, he ran with it and things snowballed. Among other things, he said he found a link between Hasbrok and Ryan. Apparently they'd conspired to make use of members of the militia Hasbrok supposedly disbanded after the tsunami."

"Did you know we had a little run-in with some of those boys while we were trying to track down Dihb Wilki?" Ferstera asked.

Alkihn nodded. "Yes, my men told me. And my guess is that we'll find out Hasbrok had more men stashed away, not just out on Weh Island."

"*Had*?" Ferstera stared at the police chief. "What are you saying? Hasbrok is dead?"

Alkihn nodded gravely. "He was shot about an hour ago."

Ferstera was incredulous. "He was at the camp?"

"No," Alkihn said. "He was shot here on the mainland. By Dujara."

"You've got to be kidding."

"I'm only telling you what I've heard," Alkihn said. "Dujara told me he went to confront Hasbrok with his findings and had a gun pulled on him. He says he managed to get the gun away and shoot Hasbrok in self-defense."

"He went to Hasbrok alone," Ferstera said, making sure he'd heard correctly. "No backup, unarmed. And Hasbrok winds up shot to death, supposedly with his own gun."

"That's his story," Alkihn said. "And my guess is Dujara will be able to supply evidence to corroborate everything he told me about Hasbrok being behind the killings in Gunung Leuser, not to mention this whole conspiracy thing with Carl Ryan."

"I'm sure you're right," Ferstera said. "And I'm sure all that evidence will be planted, just like the gun he used on Hasbrok."

"He won't get away with it," Alkihn assured the Australian. "And just so you know, I've looked into your other concerns. This mole inside the station you're looking for? The one who leaked the names of Dihb Wilki's contacts to the men you encountered at that cabin? It's not one of my people."

"Dujara," Ferstera said as it all came together.

"He has security clearance here," Alkihn explained. "Getting those names would have been no problem for him. And, I can assure you, we'll find a link between him and the cars those men took to the cabin, not to mention their identification papers. Who knows, with any luck, we'll be able to do it without expending a lot of manpower."

"Good luck with that," Ferstera said. "Where is Dujara now, anyway?"

"Right behind you."

Ferstera turned and looked through the opened blinds in the window separating Alkihn's office from the rest of the police station. Sinso Dujara was talking with the desk sergeant, looking comfortable in the knowledge that he'd been asked down to the station as a mere formality.

"I told him we'd just need him to sign off on a statement as to what happened with Hasbrok," Alkihn told Ferstera. "He thinks I bought his little story hook, line and sinker. A few minutes in the interrogation room and he'll find out differently."

"I'd pay to see that," Ferstera said.

"I have a better idea," Alkihn said, flashing what for him was an uncharacteristically sly grin. "I'll set him up for the takedown, then you can come in and have a ringside seat."

Java Sea

MANNING THE HELM of the stolen cabin cruiser had been easier than Ti Vohn had anticipated. She was out on the open sea and the water was calm, leaving her little to concern herself with but keeping the throttle steady and making certain that she stayed on a course that kept her within sight of the coastline. She had friends and relatives in Surabaya as well as on the islands of Bali and Lombok. She felt that several of them were trustworthy enough to take her in without asking too many questions. All she had to do was make contact and arrange to be picked up once she brought the boat back to shore. Things would get tricky at that point, but she thought she'd be able maneuver the boat to a dock back. The greater—and more immediate—problem was getting in touch with her benefactors.

She had turned off the boat's two-way radio and wasn't about to use it, wary that its signal might somehow tip off her position to those looking for her. Instead, she'd relied on her cell phone. She was getting a strong signal, but no one answered when she made her first few calls, forcing her to leave messages. Her frustration escalated once she noticed that the phone's battery was running low.

She pinned her final hope on an old boyfriend in Jakarta. She dialed the number then tensed as she heard the call go through. On the third ring, she got an answer.

Her hopes spiked when she recognized the voice.

"Graito!" she said, speaking quickly. "It's Ti Vohn. Please, listen to me carefully. I'm in a boat heading your—"

The phone went dead.

Beside herself, she fought back tears as she tried to turn the phone back on.

Nothing.

It was all she could do not to fling the phone against the nearest wall. She'd been so close to finding a way out of her dilemma, yet now here she was, thrown back into the grips of uncertainty. If only she'd been able to stay on the line a few minutes longer…

She suddenly realized there was still hope. Idling the boat's engines, she ventured from the helm to the bathroom. Dihb Wilki was where she'd left him, dead on the floor. She knew at some point she would have to get rid of the body and clean the mess, but she'd held off, and now she was grateful she had.

Doing her best to avoid looking at the dead man's grotesque visage, she crouched and went through his pockets until she found his cell phone. She turned it on as she headed back to the helm. The battery was only one bar shy of being fully charged.

She quickly dialed her friend's number. The call went directly to voice mail. She realized Graito was probably trying to call her back on her dead phone. When prompted to leave a message, she hurriedly explained, "Graito! I'm on another phone! When you get this message, call back the number listed! Please! It's urgent!"

She hung up but left the phone turned on. Graito would call back. He had to, she told herself.

As she waited, she opened up the throttle and forged ahead through the dark, placid waters. She'd decided she would continue making her way toward Lombok. If Graito came through, great. If not, she'd try a few other people. Once she knew for sure where she was headed, she'd haul Wilki up to the deck and heave him overboard, the same way he'd done with the boat's owner back in Banda Aceh. She'd clean the bathroom and there would be no trace left of him.

She began to formulate a cover story for Graito or whoever she wound up turning to for help. She was still working out the details when the phone rang. She quickly grabbed it.

"Hello," she said. "Graito?"

There was no response at first, then Vohn heard a voice that made her blood run cold.

"It's you," Agmed Hasem said. "What happened to Wilki?"

Vohn let out an involuntary cry and cast the phone away in horror. It fell to the floor and the LED display went black, leaving the woman back where she'd been before she'd taken the phone off Wilki's body. The only difference was that now she'd aroused the suspicions—and no doubt the ire—of the one man she feared more than any other.

Makassar, Sulawesi, Indonesia

AGMED HASEM was in a rage. For once, he realized it, and rather than cave in to his usual instinct to lash out at the first available target, he left the Quonset hut that served as his headquarters and roamed the moonlit grounds of the former treatment plant. The guards posted about the perimeter knew from experience that if Hasem was out and about at this hour it was never a good thing, and as such they did their best to look vigilant and avoid meeting his gaze. Hasem ignored them, lost in thought, searching for the best way to deal with his situation.

He was certain Ti Vohn had somehow found out what Dihb Wilki had in store for her. It seemed unlikely he would allow her to use his phone or that she'd been able to steal it without his realizing it. Most likely she'd overpowered him somehow or perhaps even killed him. Either way, Hasem knew that his former lover had no intention of coming to Makassar. He was just as certain that there was no way he could allow her to remain free. Whatever it took, he was going to track her down.

The Jemaah Islamiyah leader's ambling inevitably brought him past the holding tanks and up to the top of the small mountain overlooking his camp. There were two sentries posted on the mountaintop, which afforded an unobstructed view in all directions. The sentries, unable to ignore Hasem's presence, reported no suspicious activity.

"Quiet!" he told them. "I need to think!"

The sentries fell silent and turned away. Hasem took in the panoramic view as he continued to grasp for options. A few miles to the north, Makassar's scattered lights winked in the night. Beyond the city lay the vast strait separating Sulawesi from Borneo. Elsewhere there was little to see but an endless range of forested wilderness threaded by narrow, two-lane roads. Between the camp and city, however, a private airfield had been carved out of the woods. Several small planes were out on the tarmac next to a darkened hangar. A three-story high control tower stood next to the runway. Sprouting up next to it was an even taller tower topped with a cluster of antennae. Under the guise of a shadow corporation based in Makassar, Hasem had surreptitiously helped pay for one of the receptors, a cell phone relay tower needed to extend a signal as far as the training camp.

Hasem's gaze lingered once it fell on the relay tower. Slowly, an idea came to him, changing his expression from frustration to one of hope.

"That's it!" he suddenly exclaimed.

The sentries glanced at him questioningly. He paid them no mind. Turning, he headed back down to the camp, taking long strides, reining in his desire to break in to a full run.

A few minutes later, Hasem had entered the vast room

inside the treatment plant where his recruits slept on foam pads spread across the floor. When he switched on the light, the men stirred, then began to stagger to their feet, wary they were about to be sent out on the dreaded night drills Hasem was known to periodically insist upon.

"Listen to me carefully," he told them. "I want you to consult among yourselves and determine which of you has the most expertise with computers. I'm looking specifically for someone who can call up whatever program I'll need to be able to pick up the GPS signal in a specific cell phone."

Weh Island

"THAT'S ONE LESS THING for us to have to deal with," Mack Bolan said, speaking over a secured line with Barbara Price. The Stony Man mission controller had just informed Bolan of Sinso Dujara's arrest for the murder of Anhi Hasbrok.

The Executioner had just met with Weh Island police officers who'd discovered the bodies of a man and a woman at an isolated cabin three miles downhill from the GAM militia camp he and Kissinger had raided several hours before.

"There's a disabled Land Rover here," Bolan reported. "We're thinking Ryan made it this far, then killed the people here to get his hands on another getaway vehicle."

"Are there any identification papers?" Price asked.

"The police are breaking in to the car as we speak," Bolan said. "Once they get to the glove compartment, I hope we'll have something."

"A name would be great," Price said. "If we run a cross-check with Ryan's likeness maybe we can find out where he's been staying."

Bolan glanced over at the vehicle. Kissinger was with the police, who'd just opened the passenger door and were working on the glove compartment.

"Any luck on Jack's end?" Bolan asked Price as he waited for the police to finish up.

"No, but...wait a second," Price said. "Akira's trying to get my attention. Hang tight."

Bolan joined Kissinger near the car. The police had just pried open the glove compartment. They withdrew a few slips of paper and looked them over. Thanks to Shelby Ferstera, the chief of police had already arranged for Bolan to have clearance regarding access to evidence, so they handed the papers to him. He was looking them over when Price came back on the line.

"Wherever Ryan is now," she reported, "he apparently has access to a computer."

"How do you know that?" Bolan wanted to know.

"His mock execution has just been posted on the Internet."

19

Makassar, Sulawesi

"What is this!?" Agmed Hasem exclaimed, eyes on the computer screen.

"I'm not sure," the terrified recruit hunched over the laptop said. Hasem's computer had not been damaged as badly as he'd feared and the recruit had been able to start it up with little difficulty. Hasem had just entered his password, calling up a home page divided into numerous boxes, including one designated for recent activity involving Jemaah Islamiyah. The field leader was staring at a picture within the latter box. It was a still frame from a video depicting a hooded figure standing before a disconsolate Carl Ryan. The figure was holding a scimitar and staring directly into the camera. The adjacent headline read: Jemaah Islamiyah Broadcasts Execution of Former U.S. Ambassador.

Hasem wasn't the only member of the JI hierarchy startled by the Web posting. He was about to tell the recruit to play the footage when his cell phone rang. It was one of his superiors, calling from a command post in East Timor. The man referenced the beheading and demanded to know, "Was this your doing?"

"I don't know anything about it!" Hasem exclaimed.

"I've checked with everyone in the chain of command," the other man retorted. "No one is owning up to it!"

"It wasn't me!" Hasem insisted. "I haven't even had a chance to view the footage."

"Someone is lying, then."

"Why would they lie?" Hasem wanted to know. "If I'd done this, I'd be more than willing to take credit!"

"Is that so?" came the reply. "Even if you'd done it without authorization?"

"It wasn't me!" Hasem repeated.

The line went dead. Hasem could feel his pulse racing. The last thing he needed was to have his superiors placing him under close scrutiny, even if it was for the wrong reason. He tried to put the matter out of his mind, telling himself it was nothing he had control over. Unless, of course, in watching the video he could glean some hint as to which of his counterparts was responsible. If he could see to it that the finger was pointed elsewhere, he would be free to proceed with his efforts to track down Vohn. For now, though, Hasem put aside his concerns over finding out if Dihb Wilki's cell phone was still transmitting a GPS signal. At the moment, like countless millions throughout cyberspace who'd chanced upon the Web posting, Hasem had given himself over to morbid curiosity.

"Play it," he told the recruit.

Hasem watched as the hooded figure unleashed a lengthy diatribe against the United States, invoking numerous clichés and stock phrases that were part of Jemaah Islamiyah's standard repertoire. Hasem only half-listened; his attention was more on the speaker and the hooded men who flanked Ryan, brandishing carbines. He didn't recognize the man's voice and no one displayed any physical trait or mannerism that reminded him of anyone in JI's chain of command. Likewise, there was nothing in the setting—a mere chair set against a blank wall—to give any indication where the execution had taken place.

Once the speaker finished his rant, he stepped to one side and the camera moved in closer to Carl Ryan. The former ambassador stared into the camera, a look of tired fear on his face. With a voice devoid of emotion, he stated his name and his former position with the U.S. government, then began to recite what was clearly a memorized speech.

"I am being held captive by Jemaah Islamiyah," Ryan said. "They have shown me no mistreatment and in speaking with them, I have come to understand the validity of their positions, especially with regards to the evildoers in the American White House and…"

Ryan stopped speaking and his face flushed with sudden anger.

"I won't do it!" he suddenly bellowed, not only at the camera but also at the men standing on either side of him. "To hell with you! You're all animals and deserve whatever we can do to see that you're wiped off the face of—"

Ryan's tirade was cut short when one of the men guarding him lashed out with the butt of his carbine, striking the former ambassador in the base of the skull with so much force that he was flung forward off his chair, dropping out of the camera's frame. The image wobbled slightly as the cameraman apparently took a step back in reaction to the disturbance. When he finally managed to pan down to the floor, Ryan came back into view, lying facedown on the floor, unconscious. When the men who'd been guarding him stepped forward, the swordsman waved them away, then chanted a keening oath and brought the blade down hard on Ryan's neck. The camera caught the head falling away from Ryan's body, then focused on the bloodied blade of the scimitar as its wielder held it aloft and then pointed it at the camera.

"Death to the blasphemer!" he shouted. "Death to the Great Satan! Rise up, and stamp out the scourge of Islam!"

The screen faded to black, then reverted to the initial freeze frame. The recruit, clearly shaken by what he'd just seen, looked up warily at Hasem, whose expression was blank. He continued to stare at the screen.

"Play it again," Hasem told the recruit. "And if there's a way to slow it down, when I tell you, do it."

Stony Man Farm

THE CYBER TEAM at Stony Man Farm was dissecting the video footage of the execution. "Okay, there!" Hal Brognola said, getting Akira Tokaido to pause the sequence just as the man to Carl Ryan's left was about to smack the former ambassador with the butt of his carbine. "Now zoom in and run it in slow motion."

All eyes were on one of the large monitors on the far wall. Tokaido, Brognola, Barbara Price, Aaron Kurtzman, Huntington Wethers and Carmen Delahunt watched as Ryan reeled from the supposed blow to his head. When viewed at a reduced speed, however, it was clear that things were not as they seemed.

"See?" Brognola said, pointing at the screen. "Ryan's in motion before the rifle connects."

"Hollywood Stunt Work 101," Kurtzman drawled. "They faked it."

The assembled group continued to watch the slow-playing footage as Ryan dropped out of the frame and the videotaped image began to wobble.

"Now Ryan's probably on his hands and knees, scrambling past the guy laid out on the floor where he supposedly fell," Brognola said. Once the camera panned down to the motionless figure on the floor, the big Fed continued, "Now we're looking at his stand-in."

"I'm sure that's it," Price agreed. She turned to Tokaido. "We don't need to see the rest."

"Fine by me," Tokaido said, blanking the screen.

Brognola turned to the others. "Obviously, the plan was to get rid of the body, then post the footage so it'd look like Ryan was out of the picture once and for all."

"Nice try," Delahunt said. "And, who knows, if Striker hadn't crashed the party, it might have worked."

"That's the part I don't get," Tokaido said. "Ryan has to know we found the body, so why bother posting the footage? The people he needed to fool are on to him."

"True," Brognola said, "but by the time somebody comes out saying it's a fraud, a few million people will have seen it and drawn their own conclusions."

"More like a few *hundred* million people," Kurtzman estimated.

"Could be," Brognola conceded. "And a good chunk of them aren't going to buy the idea it was staged. They'll think we're trying to cover up something."

"In other words," Huntington Wethers chimed in, "Ryan was just poking the hornet's nest to stir things up and buy himself some time."

Brognola nodded. "The question is, will it work?"

"I think we're about to find out," Delahunt said. She'd turned her eyes back to her own computer. "I just got a cross-reference on the name Ryan used to sign off on that rental car he ditched. 'Al Lansford' rented a condo on Gapang Bay two days after Ryan flew to Weh Island."

"Well done," Brognola told the red-haired computer wiz. "Get word to Striker, pronto."

"Speed-dialing as we speak," Delahunt said. She was already donning her headset, ready to give the Executioner the news.

Brognola turned to Wethers. "Check on the sat-cams, Hunt. The sooner we can get an eye-in-the-sky trained on Gapang Bay, the better."

Surabaya, Java

THE HUEY MEDEVAC CHOPPER entrusted to Jack Grimaldi had held up well through two refuelings, but by the time he was approaching the Indonesian navy's Eastern Armada base in

Surabaya, the Stony Man pilot felt the bird's endurance had been pushed to its limit.

Shortly after touching down, a maintenance check turned up signs of engine fatigue as well as stress fractures in the fuel line and rotor housing. As the mechanics put it, Grimaldi and his colleagues were lucky the Huey hadn't died on them. Using the aircraft to continue their search for Dihb Wilki and Ti Vohn was out of the question.

When Grimaldi got nowhere in his attempt to secure the use of a replacement chopper, he put a call through to Shelby Ferstera back in Banda Aceh. Ferstera quickly brought him up to date on Sinso Dujara's arrest for the murder of Anhi Hasbrok, then said he'd try to cut through the red tape and get Grimaldi back in the air. As he waited, Grimaldi grabbed a quick bite at the base mess hall with Muhtar Yeilam and the Indonesian soldier rounding out their search party. Afterwards he touched base with Barbara Price back at Stony Man Farm and learned that Bolan and Kissinger were apparently close to tracking down Carl Ryan on Weh Island.

As for Wilki and Vohn, Price told Grimaldi there had thus far been three sightings of cabin cruisers matching the description of the one stolen by the JI sympathizers. All three sightings had been to the south, on the other side of the islands in the Indian Ocean, and in each instance Indonesian authorities had intercepted the craft in question, only to learn that the fugitives were not on board.

"Something just came in from Marunda, though," Price informed Grimaldi. "A store clerk claims she sold a few things to a couple of customers matching the description. One of the things they bought was antinausea medication."

"If it was them, then it seems a lock they were headed back out to sea," Grimaldi said.

"That's our take," Price agreed. "We've run checks and

they both have known contacts in Java as well as the islands just east of there."

"Then either we've passed them already or we're on their tail," Grimaldi said.

"Let's hope it's the latter," Price said.

"Maybe not," Grimaldi replied. He told the mission controller about the loaner Huey being grounded and his difficulty securing a replacement.

"I wouldn't worry about that," Price assured him. "We're patched in with Ferstera for the time being. If he needs a little extra clout, we'll weigh in and make sure you're good to go."

Grimaldi chuckled. "Too bad you guys weren't around back when I was sending Christmas wishes to the North Pole," he said. "I'd have had a hell of a lot happier childhood."

Once he was off the call, Grimaldi took a short walk around some of the outbuildings, welcoming the chance for a little exercise and fresh air after all the hours he'd spent holed up in the Huey's cockpit. When he caught up with the others, Muhtar Yeilam was having a discussion with the same officer who'd balked earlier at letting them use a replacement chopper.

"He wants to know which we'd prefer," Yeilam told Grimaldi when the flyboy joined him, "A Blackhawk or Apache..."

Makassar, Sulawesi

"CAN'T YOU DO THIS any faster?" Agmed Hasem screamed.

"I almost have it," the recruit said, quickly adding, "sir."

Both men were staring at the laptop computer in Hasem's headquarters. They'd turned their attention away from the execution video and were now focused on pinpointing the GPS signal emanating from Dihb Wilki's cell phone. The recruit had already logged the longitude and latitude and was waiting for the computer to finish zooming in on a satellite image corresponding with the coordinates.

At first it appeared that the signal was coming from the open sea five miles from the northern coast of Lombok, but as the image magnified, a faint scattering of dots began to show up on the screen.

"Islands?" Hasem asked.

"Smaller than that," the recruit said. "They look more like coral formations."

The Web site image was dated, so there was no chance of spotting the stolen cabin cruiser, and there came a point after which the zoom function cancelled out and a message flashed on the screen confirming that a closer view was unobtainable. The recruit zoomed back until the ocean view came back on the screen.

"Switch back to the GPS site," Hasem said.

The recruit obliged, then quickly checked the readings being sent out by Wilki's cell phone.

"No change," the recruit said. "The boat hasn't moved."

"Then she's either anchored there or she's run aground," Hasem speculated. He'd already been formulating a plan and he decided it was time to put it in motion. He went to the cabinet next to his desk and withdrew two assault rifles, then pointed to a radio transceiver on the table next to the computer.

"Keep monitoring the signal," Hasem told the recruit. "Radio me if there's a change."

"Yes, sir."

Hasem strode from the hut. Four of his senior aides were standing nearby, waiting on his orders. He handed an assault rifle to one of them, then motioned to one of the large holding tanks situated behind the treatment plant.

"Help me get the tarp off," he told them.

Hasem led the way to the larger of the tanks. When they reached it, the men spread out, untying the binds that secured the massive camouflage tarpaulin draped over the top. Once the tarp was untethered, the men pulled it clear. Hasem gave some last-minute instructions to two of his men, then gestured for the others to follow him up the ladder rungs welded to the tank's side. Once they cleared the rim, they took a second set of rungs down into the tank, which had been empty for years.

Set in the middle of the massive drum was a stripped-down OH-6 Cayuse, a long-range reconnaissance helicopter Hasem had refurbished after purchasing it at a salvage auction. Shed of armaments and excess weight, the chopper had enough range to reach Vohn without the need to refuel.

Less than five minutes later, a deafening roar echoed off the walls of the holding tank as the helicopter's engine coughed to life. The overhead rotor stirred up a cloud of dust that all but engulfed the chopper. Riding shotgun beside the pilot, Hasem clenched his assault rifle as the bird rose through the cloud and then drifted past the camp, heading south for the Java Sea and his long-awaited reunion with the only woman ever to have turned her back on him.

Finally, he would have a chance to show her the error of her ways.

20

Gapang Bay, Weh Island

"His computer's here, along with the video camera," Bolan reported, "and the truck he stole is parked down the block. No sign of Ryan, though."

The Executioner was standing in the living room of Carl Ryan's beachfront condo, Beretta in hand, cell phone to his ear. He and Kissinger had broken in and searched all three floors. Kissinger was out on the balcony, completing a second sweep. Bolan had just called Hal Brognola but the big Fed was a step ahead of him.

"Ryan's out in the bay," Brognola said.

"How can you be sure?" Bolan asked.

"Sat-cam," Brognola explained. "We've got an orbiter trained on the area, and they picked up a boat anchored about a half mile out. Same make as the rental boat Ryan charged on his forged credit card."

"Sounds like you guys are working overtime," Bolan said.

"You know it," Brognola replied. "There's no one in the boat and Ryan bought scuba gear, so he has to be in the water. And if you ask me, he's not looking to escape to Atlantis."

"He's after the tsunami funds," Bolan guessed.

"If that's the case, he converted it to something he could hide underwater."

"Got it," said Bolan. "We'll take it from here."

"One more thing," Brognola cautioned. "Ryan also bought a speargun."

"Understood." The Executioner hung up just as Kissinger was coming in from the balcony.

"He's got a turtle shell curing on the wall," Kissinger said, "but that's about it."

"Could you see a marina or some kind of docks from out there?" Bolan asked.

"Yeah, why?"

"We need to borrow a boat...."

ALONG WITH HIS SPEARGUN, Carl Ryan had an underwater torch. Focusing its concentrated flame, he was burning his way through one of the flat steel bars protecting the water-proof container securely wedged into its hiding place beneath the coral ledge located in the deep waters of Gapang Bay.

The fugitive had been relieved to find the container undisturbed. When he'd seen that Anhi Hasbrok's cabin cruiser was missing from its slip, he'd feared the worst. He wasn't sure of the GAM leader's whereabouts, and at this point he didn't much care. All that mattered to Ryan was retrieving the container and getting back to his boat as quickly as possible. He wasn't sure of his next move, but he knew it would be too risky to return to his condominium. He felt he'd been lucky to have enough time to post the footage of his supposed execution without his pursuers catching up with him.

Ryan figured his best bet was to head out from the bay and circle the island, seeking a larger boat or some other avenue of escape. The sooner he could leave Weh behind and find safe refuge elsewhere, the sooner he could check to see how much chaos the video had unleashed. Any diversion would likely allow him the time he'd need to regroup. Ryan was resigned to the idea that he would have to wait far longer than antici-pated before going after his successor in Jakarta, but he remained determined that, with or without Hasbrok's help, the day would come when he would have his vengeance on Ambassador Gardner.

Ryan's torch flame was bright enough that he was able to keep his flashlight clipped to his scuba belt. The flickering illumination had the disadvantage, however, of drawing the attention of countless underwater species. Several times he'd been interrupted by the need to wave away schools of small fish, and in another instance he'd had to aim the torch at an overly inquisitive eel to convince it to retreat back to its lair.

Now, just as he was about to finish cutting through the first of the steel bars, Ryan was interrupted yet again, this time by the approach of a slow-moving box jellyfish. Tentacles dangling from its basketball-sized frame, the luminous invertebrate looked harmless enough, but Ryan knew it was, in fact, one of the most poisonous creatures on the planet. There was no way he could turn his back in hopes the beast would leave him alone.

More annoyed than alarmed, Ryan dimmed his torch and wedged it in the coral, then unslung his speargun and quickly unfastened the line affixed to its barbed shaft. He took careful aim and once the jellyfish had drawn to within five yards of him, he triggered the gun. A barbed spear rocketed forth, plunging clear through the creature's gelatinous body. Tentacles flailing, the predator fell away from Ryan and sank into the depths extending far below the coral shelf.

The danger behind him, Ryan recharged the gun and fitted it with a fresh spear, then slung it back over his shoulder. He retrieved the torch and went back to work on the bars, hopeful he'd had to contend with his last distraction.

DAWN WAS BREAKING when the Executioner emerged from the darkened supply shop located on the dock assigned to tenants at Carl Ryan's condominium complex. He had changed into a wet suit and was carrying scuba gear along

with a speargun. Farther down the dock, Kissinger had just
hot-wired a small, twin-engine catamaran and was poised at
the helm. Bolan quickly untied the boat's mooring line and
climbed aboard before pushing away from the dock.

"I figure we're up to about a half-dozen felonies by now,"
Kissinger quipped as he opened the throttles and navigated
the catamaran out into the bay.

"I think some of them are just misdemeanors," Bolan said.

It wasn't the first time circumstances had required the
Stony Man ops to break the law, and Bolan knew it wouldn't
be the last. He also knew that Hal Brognola would see to it
that the owners of the boat and supply shop were adequately
compensated for their involuntary assistance in the mission.

"You don't plan on using that flashlight, do you?" Kissinger asked, noting the equipment clipped to the scuba belt
Bolan was strapping on.

"Only as a last resort," Bolan said. "The sun's coming up,
so I should be good enough for the first thirty feet or so. After
that, we'll see."

"Or not," Kissinger said. "And from what they found out
at the Farm, it sounds like Ryan knows his way around down
there. He'll have the home-court advantage."

"I don't have any control over that," Bolan said. "As long as
it's just him down there, I'll take my chances going one-on-one."

Java Sea

THE FOG WAS BEGINNING to let up by the time Ti Vohn had dragged Dihb Wilki's stiffening corpse up onto the deck of the cabin cruiser. As she stopped to catch her breath, sweating from the exertion, she glanced past the forward bow. In the predawn light she could now see at least a dozen places where coral rose above the waterline. No wonder she'd run aground, she thought. The largest formation, thirty yards away, was roughly the size of a baseball diamond, level in spots but otherwise crowned by raised, towerlike spires splattered with guano. A pair of sea lions had hauled themselves onto the makeshift island, and when they spotted her they began to yelp. Their barks echoed loudly across the water, rattling the woman's frayed nerves.

"Shut up!" she shouted at them, to no avail.

Turning back to her grisly task, she bent over and looked away from Wilki's ravaged face as she grabbed him under the armpits. Straining, she lifted the body and propped it against the side of the boat long enough to shift her grip and grab one of the dead man's legs. Once she could feel his weight balanced on the railing, she heaved with all her might. Wilki tumbled over the side and splashed loudly into the water. Ti Vohn stared over the side and saw that the body was still visible, sprawled across the coral only a few feet below the waterline.

As she cursed and leaned against the side of the boat, she knew she had to be rid of any trace of Wilki so that she could place a distress call. If she could be rescued by someone unaware she was a fugitive, she figured she could charm her way ashore and still have a chance to put this nightmare behind her.

Although the cabin cruiser was firmly aground on the coral, the boat still moved slightly in the gentle surf, and when she heard the anchorline slap faintly against the hull, she had a flash of inspiration. Walking across the blood-streaked deck, she went to the galley, where she'd remembered seeing a large knife. The knife's blade was sharp and serrated, and once she brought it back out onto the deck she began to saw at the anchorline. It took more effort than she'd expected, but finally the blade cut through.

Holding the end of the rope still connected to the anchor, Vohn moved to the outer ladder and slowly lowered herself until she was standing on the coral, the water up to her waist. More sea lions had bellied up onto the coral island, joining their counterparts in a noisy chorus. Vohn ignored the un-nerving racket as best she could and slowly pulled in the an-chorline. Soon the anchor came into view, carrying with it the snagged remains of a kelp bed.

Once she'd pried away the kelp, she drew in a deep breath and dropped under the water. Working quickly, she wound the thick line around Wilki's torso several times, then wedged the anchor between the rope and the corpse. She looped the re-maining slack around Wilki's neck before tying the loose end into a half hitch close to the anchor. She was running out of air, so she surfaced long enough to fill her lungs, then went back under. It took all her strength to roll the body away from the boat. Finally it toppled free of the coral. Weighed down by the anchor, Dihb Wilki sank quickly, vanishing into the depths.

Vohn rose to her feet and leaned against the side of the boat,

eyes closed, gasping for air. Her ears were plugged, and it
wasn't until the water had drained from them that she realized
the braying of the sea lions had been replaced by an even
louder and more persistent sound.

Opening her eyes, she saw that a helicopter had just landed
on the coral island. The chopper was turned away from her,
its rotors still whirring, scattering the startled sea lions back
into the water.

Ti Vohn froze. She wasn't sure how they'd found her, but
she was being rescued too soon. She'd just disposed of the
body, but the boat still bore traces of foul play.

Keep them away, she told herself. She moved away from
the cabin cruiser, waving her arms instinctively, her mind
racing for plausible cover stories should she be unable to
prevent her rescuers from looking the boat over.

She had taken only a few steps when she suddenly stopped
in her tracks and stared in horror at the helicopter. The cockpit
door opened and a man brandishing an assault rifle stepped
out onto the coral.

"LONG TIME, NO SEE, my love," Agmed Hasem called out.
"Have you missed me as much as I missed you?"

Vohn stared at him, wild-eyed and silent. When she turned
and began to climb up toward the deck of the cabin cruiser,
Hasem calmly raised his assault rifle and took aim. He held
back from pulling the trigger, however.

"No," he whispered to himself. "That would be too easy."

Lowering the carbine, Hasem ventured to the edge of the
coral island. It would be possible to wade to the next formation, but beyond that he would have to swim to reach the boat.
He decided against it and retreated to the chopper, ducking
low to avoid the rotors. He exchanged a few words with the
pilot and the gunman riding beside him, then stood on the
chopper's strut and held onto the door frame with one hand

as the bird lifted off. As he was carried over the coral formations, he kept an eye on Vohn, who'd climbed aboard the cabin cruiser and was heading below. He could see blood on the deck and assumed it was Wilki's.

"Nice try," he murmured. "You almost got away with it."

The helicopter was within thirty yards of the cabin cruiser when Vohn reappeared on the deck. She had a pistol in her hand, and before Hasem could bring his assault rifle into play, she fired a stream of bullets at the chopper. Two of them nailed Hasem, one in the ribs, the other in the arm that was holding onto the Cayuse's door frame. Howling in pain, the JI commando lost his grip and fell.

VOHN HOBBLED TO the railing. Hasem had landed in the water between the cabin cruiser and the nearest coral formation. He was still alive, clutching his assault rifle as he tried to tread water with his wounded arm. She took aim, determined to finish him off.

She was about to shoot when a rattle of gunfire sounded from the helicopter. One of the shots tore through her hip. Her leg gave out on her and she crumpled to the deck. Frantic, she crawled away from the railing, sliding through Wilki's blood. She was struck four more times before she reached the cabin. Bullets pounded into the framework, shattering glass and stinging her with shrapnel as she dragged herself down into the sleeping quarters. She pulled at a blanket and drew it around her, curling into a fetal position on the floor.

"Bastard," she said. The defiance was gone from her voice, however.

A moment later, she was silent.

SHOCK, RAGE AND ADRENALINE all combined to numb Agmed Hasem to the pain radiating from his bullet-torn arm. Relying on leg kicks, he slowly made his way through the cold dawn water until he reached the coral formation where the cabin cruiser had beached. Once he was able to stand on the coral, he slung the carbine over his shoulder and used his one good arm to grab hold of the boat's ladder.

The gunfire coming from the helicopter ceased once he'd made it up to the bullet-riddled deck. The droning of the Cayuse's rotors matched the pulsing in Hasem's temples as he planted his feet on the blood-soaked planks and looked around. Vohn was nowhere to be seen, but she'd left a clear trail. Hasem took a step, then stopped as he spotted a large knife on the deck. He picked it up, grinning mercilessly. It would serve his purposes much better than the assault rifle. He wanted Ti Vohn's death to be as slow and painful as possible.

The terrorist made his way to the sleeping quarters, knife in hand.

He was almost belowdecks when his helicopter suddenly erupted in a fireball. Debris rained down on Hasem even as shockwaves from the explosion threw him off balance. He staggered to one side and slipped on the blood-slicked steps, landing hard on one knee.

Bewildered, Hasem turned and glanced over his shoulder.

Materializing out of the last wisps of fog was an Apache gunship, flying low over the water, headed directly toward him. He knew in an instant that it was over.

Determined to go down fighting, the JI leader struggled to his feet. Out over the water, the Apache ceased its approach and turned to one side. The passenger door opened, revealing an Indonesian man. He was seated next to the pilot in the cockpit, armed with an assault rifle matching Hasem's in firepower.

Hasem raised his own carbine, but before he could fire, the other man cut loose. The Makassar Madman's chest turned to confetti as the avenger's rounds tore into him. Blood bubbled up through Hasem's lips as he collapsed to the deck, choking on his final words.

22

Gapang Bay

BY THE TIME KISSINGER had eased the catamaran alongside Carl Ryan's boat, Bolan was ready to enter the water.

"Break a leg," Kissinger told him. "Or preferably not."

"If I'm not back in—"

"You'll be back," Kissinger interrupted. "I'm counting on you to smooth things over with the angry natives once we get back ashore."

"Wouldn't want to miss that," Bolan said.

Once his mouthpiece was in place, the Executioner back-flipped into the bay. The search was on.

It had been some time since Bolan's war against the enemy had taken him underwater, but he was no stranger to the element and he finned his way expertly into the briny depths. There was plenty to distract him, but he ignored the activity of the bay's natural inhabitants and remained focused, peering through his mask for some sign of Ryan. The relative darkness worked to his advantage. Within a few minutes of reaching the coral sprawl that lined the bay floor, he spotted an ambient glow that seeped out from under a ledge less than fifty yards away.

Bolan waited for a cloud of plankton to flitter past him, then made his way cautiously along the edge of the coral shelf, veering his way around a sponge-encrusted formation as well as a drifting clot of seaweed being fed upon by several schools of small fish.

Closer to the light source, Bolan ran into trouble in the form of a large octopus that had just snared a passing fish with one of its elongated limbs. The creature was territorial, mistaking Bolan for some rival predator out to steal its catch. Without releasing its hold on the grouper, the octopus pushed itself up off the coral and headed Bolan's way.

Bolan twisted in the water and changed course, but his eight-legged pursuer moved with surprising speed, and moments later the Executioner felt a firm grip around his right ankle. He tried to shake free but the beast's appendage coiled tightly like a python intent on squeezing the life from its prey and Bolan could feel himself being pulled within range of the creature's other limbs.

Left with no choice, Bolan went to his speargun, taking quick aim past the undulating extremities and firing at the sea creature's exposed eye. The shaft hit its mark, sending the octopus into death throes. It released its grip and slithered to one side before propelling itself away from its attacker, leaving an inky cloud in its wake.

The Executioner hadn't bothered with a retrieval line when he'd taken the speargun, so he was free to distance himself from the wounded creature. He swam a few yards to his left, then hovered in the water long enough to feed another spear into the gun.

He was preparing to resume his search when he realized that his altercation with the octopus has alerted the fugitive ambassador to his presence. Carl Ryan had emerged from below the coral ledge, a small container tucked under one arm. His speargun was in the other.

RYAN GLARED THROUGH HIS MASK.

The sons of bitches had caught up with him.

Temper flaring, Ryan was about to fire his speargun when

he caught himself. He only had two spears and the diver was too far out of range to waste a shot.

You want me, come and get me, he thought. Moving backward, Ryan dropped from the coral and sank below the ledge. He'd left his torch in the cavity where his tsunami plunder had been stashed for so long. Grabbing the tool, he quickly activated the flame, then set it back in the opening and swam farther beneath the shelf, still clutching the waterproof container. Twenty yards ahead, he knew there was a break in the shelf he could squeeze through, placing himself back above the coral. If, as he hoped, his pursuer were to stop at the ledge near where he'd set the torch, Ryan would be able to come up on him from behind and put a spear through his back.

THE EXECUTIONER was nearing the ledge where Ryan had been positioned when he suddenly stopped.

His instincts were screaming that Ryan had set a trap.

Ryan had nothing to gain by going deeper into the water. Sooner or later he'd run low on air and would have to make his way to the surface, so the only reason to drop below the ledge would be to somehow catch Bolan off guard.

Bolan went with the hunch. Instead of chasing after the light, he swam the other way, seeking cover behind a coral mound allowing him to monitor the entire length of the long shelf. The next move would be up to Ryan.

AS HE ROSE UP through the crevasse, Ryan could see all the way to the surface of the bay. A catamaran was positioned directly next to his boat. Ryan didn't know if there was anyone aboard, but he didn't have enough air to try to swim his way to shore. Once he took care of his underwater pursuer, he would have to head straight up and take his chances.

The former ambassador set the container holding his fortune on the coral and wriggled up through the opening. His target was less than twenty yards away, back to him, staring out toward the ledge.

Ryan readied the speargun, took aim and pulled the trigger.

IF NOT FOR HIS SCUBA GEAR, Bolan's Long War would likely have come to an end, with Gapang Bay becoming the warrior's final resting place.

The deadly shaft Ryan had hoped to plant between the Executioner's shoulder blades was deflected by the diving cylinder strapped to Bolan's back. Glancing upward, the spear still managed to pierce Bolan's wetsuit and graze his shoulder, but the wound wasn't severe.

Wincing, Bolan threw himself against the coral mound, then pushed off, kicking with his fins to generate enough momentum to distance himself from the spot where he'd nearly met his maker. In the same motion, he torqued his body, turning around so that he could get a glimpse of his attacker. Ryan was already loading a second bolt into his speargun.

Bolan swung his own gun into position. The moment he landed back on the coral, he steadied his aim and unleashed a spear of his own. Ryan was facing him, so there was no tank to shield him. Bolan's shot whizzed past the fugitive's raised speargun and penetrated his wetsuit.

Ryan dropped his speargun and instinctively grabbed at the shaft protruding from his chest. Trying to work the spear free, he inadvertently jerked its barbed edge through one of the arteries leading to his heart and he began to bleed profusely. Bolan watched as the man's weighted scuba belt pulled him down onto the coral. Ryan's right hand came to rest only a few inches from the waterproof container he'd just collected.

When Bolan reached the body, he leaned over and picked up the container. He wasn't about to try to break the seal while he was still underwater, but when he shook the box he could feel the stone-like rattle of its contents and guessed that Ryan had converted his tsunami plunder into precious stones. How fitting, Bolan thought, for the plunderer to have met his demise in the same waters that had brought him his ill-gotten gain.

Justice had been served....

23

Stony Man Farm

"DENSUS 88 TRACED HASEM back to a training camp in Makassar," Brognola explained. "The place was deserted, though. Ferstera figures his men scattered like rats and will probably hook up with other cells."

"I'm sure he'll track them down," Bolan said.

The two men were seated in the old War Room back at the Farm's main house. Bolan's arm was in a sling.

"Ferstera sends his regards, by the way," Brognola said. "He hopes you'll make it back out there some day so you two can compare scars."

"I just might take him up on that," Bolan replied.

Brognola grinned. "I'm sure you'll do the same crappy job of following doctor's orders as he did. They tell him to take a few weeks off, he's back at it in two days."

"Can't keep a good man down," Bolan said.

"Funny, that's the same line Zailik's using now that it looks like he's a shoo-in for reelection," Brognola said.

"Good for him," Bolan replied. "And if he fast-tracks that housing project with those tsunami funds we dropped in his lap, he won't have to worry about the reception he gets next time he takes the back way to the airport."

Barbara Price entered the room, toting a clipboard stacked with dispatches and logistical papers related to an assignment involving the Farm's two commando teams, Phoenix Force and Able Team.

"The guys are ready to be briefed over at the Annex," she told Brognola.

The big Fed rose and held out his hand for the clipboard. "Why don't you let me go ahead and handle it."

"That's all right," Price said.

"I insist," Brognola replied.

Price handed over the notes. Brognola grinned at his colleagues, then headed out into the corridor, leaving Bolan alone with Price for the first time since he'd returned from Indonesia.

"Subtlety was never his strong suit," Bolan said.

Price closed the door and threw the dead bolt, then turned to the Executioner, smiling seductively. "Mine, either," she said.

TAKE 'EM FREE
2 action-packed novels plus a mystery bonus
NO RISK
NO OBLIGATION TO BUY

JAMES AXLER

DEATH LANDS

Desolation Crossing

Survive or perish in a world gone hideously wrong....

The legend of the trader returns in the simmering dust bowl of the Badlands, the past calling out to Armorer J. B. Dix. Her name is Eula, young, silent, lethal and part of a new trading convoy quick to invite Ryan Cawdor and his band on a journey across the hostile terrain. But high-tech hardware and friendly words don't tell the real story behind a vendetta that is years in the making.

Available July wherever books are sold.

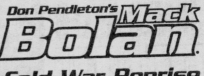

James Axler
Outlanders®

JANUS TRAP

Earth's last line of defense is invaded by a revitalized and reconfigured foe....

The Original Tribe, technological shamans with their own agenda of domination, challenged Cerberus once before and lost. Now their greatest assassin, Broken Ghost, has trapped the original Cerberus warriors in a matrix of unreality and altering protocols. As Broken Ghost destabilizes Earth's great defense force from within, the true warriors struggle to regain a foothold back to the only reality that offers survival....

Available August wherever books are sold.

AleX Archer
SEEKER'S CURSE

In Nepal, many things are sacred. And worth killing for.

Enlisted by the Japan Buddhist Federation to catalog a number of ancient shrines across Nepal, Annja is their last hope to properly conserve these sites. As vandalism and plundering occur, police become suspicious of Annja—but she's more concerned with the smugglers and guerrillas trying to kill her. As she treks high into the Himalayas to protect a sacred statue, she's told the place is cursed. But Annja has no choice but to face the demons....

Available July wherever books are sold.

GOLD EAGLE®